Trickster:

Myths from the Ahtna Indians of Alaska

Trickster:
Myths from the Ahtna Indians of Alaska

Compiled & Edited
John Smelcer

Foreword by Gary Snyder

Naciketas Press
715 E. McPherson
Kirksville, Missouri 63501
2016

Trickster ©2016 John Smelcer
Illustrations by Larry Vienneau. Cover design by Rusty Nelson.

ISBN   978-1-936135-19-6 (1-936135-19-1)

Library of Congress Control Number: 2016901616

Published by:
Naciketas Press
715 E. McPherson
Kirksville, Missouri 63501

Available at:
Nitai's Bookstore
715 E. McPherson
Kirksville, Missouri, 63501
Phone: (660) 665-0273
http://www.nitaisbookstore.com
http://www.naciketas-press.com
Email: neal@blazing-sapphire-press.com

for the Ahtna People,
Atna' Koht'aene

Contents

Foreword

Tucked back between the Chugach and the St. Elias Mountains, with the Wrangells to the east; up in the valleys and tributaries of the Copper River, and hidden south of the main route over to the Yukon drainage, is Ahtna Country. As editor John Smelcer says, perhaps the last Native group in North America to be contacted by the Euro-Americans, so remote they were. A self-sufficient and self-governing People tucked into a far corner of glaciers, mountains, and spruce woods; little seen, little known. A country that ranges from the edge of the sub-boreal taiga through peaks and canyons to the enormous ice fields of the monster coastal ranges facing the Gulf of Alaska.

This neat, compact book brings us their myths and tales. As is usually true in the world of traditional story, they are both unique to place, and also cosmopolitan. They belong to the broader realm of the Athabaskan language family that stretches from the Yukon basin to the mountains of southern Arizona, with a pocket even in coastal California. So, many of the stories are variants of widely-told tales; some even belong to the archaic international world of stories that reaches from Virginia to Finland, and down into Africa. These little family-told narratives introduce us again to "Way long ago," a place that will be familiar forever—where baby Raven plays on the dirt floor (like baby Krishna) biding his time to steal the sun, stars, and moon that are bound in the fancy boxes of his grandfather. Where the web of magic and relationship is such that Fox's daughter can be married to Raven; where kindness to a little mouse will be repaid tenfold richly in bundles of food; where the tricks can be fierce—as when the fox fools the wolves into eating their greedy sister ("You ate your sister!" he taunts) and when Raven tricks Grizzly Bear so that he can kill and eat him. This primary world of the self-governing Peoples of North America is not for sissies. The lessons are hard, but true.

Raven is the creator. He "created salmon to join the streams and rivers to the sea"—so ingenious and far-thinking he was. But his lessons are often a matter of teaching by bad, rather than by good example. The world of these tales is totally moral, but via a hard-core realism that rings honest to our actual situation—where Creation is possibly partly mischief, and we must deal with a world of complexities. But even Raven's mistakes can sometimes be poignant, as when he falls in love with a beautiful goose maiden, and try as he may, cannot keep up with her when it's time to fly south.

The Ahtna People give us again this gift of an ancient, totally present, real world where we walk with archetypal fox, rabbit, porcupine, camp-robber, bear . . . through the imagination we human beings (and maybe all the other critters too!) all share.

Gary Snyder,
University of California, Davis

Distribution of Alaska Native Cultures and Languages.

Introduction

Our stories tell much about us. They teach us who we are. They define our place in the natural world, and they establish a history, an origin for many of our beliefs, traditions, and customs. Indeed, in attempting to understand who we are, every human culture has a corpus of myth by which to understand existence. The thirty-three stories in this book represent the most complete collection of our stories ever assembled. They come from the Ahtna people themselves—from interviews, historical records and notes, and from previously printed material.

While many Native tribes in the continental United States no longer live on traditionally-ancestral lands because they were displaced by the American government in previous centuries, no Alaska Native Peoples have been so removed. For the most part, our tribes and villages are in the same geographic region they have existed in for hundreds, perhaps even thousands of years. We are a people tied to our land. In many ways this union defines our very lives—the way we view the land, subsist from it, and how we teach our children these values. Even our language is influenced by geography.

The Ahtna People were perhaps the last Indian tribe in North America contacted by Europeans. As an inland Athabaskan culture, we lived in a country untouched and unimpacted from outside non-Native influences until 1885 when Lt. Henry Allen first made his way, torturously at times, into the heart of our country. The first wave of outsiders didn't really occur until the late 1890's, during the Klondike Gold Rush made famous by Jack London.

Archaeologists suggest that we Ahtna have lived in this region, in *Atna' Nen'*—Ahtna country—for thousands of years. In that time we named every place in the country; every stream, creek, river, and lake.

Every mountain, hill, and bluff has a name that our ancestors gave to it. Two predominant landmarks define our country: the Wrangell St. Elias mountain range and the Copper River. Our very name comes from the latter (*Atna' Tuu*). For countless generations we have lived along the edge of the Copper River and its tributaries, and we have lived and died in the shadows of those mountains—mountains which have borne Indian names throughout the memory of a People. In the Ahtna language we call Mt. Drum, Mt. Sanford, and Mt. Wrangell: K'elt'aeni, Hwniidi K'elt'aeni, and Hwdaandi Kelt'aeni. After contact, however, the old names were lost to new names given to our country, names given by newcomers with no history on the land, and in a new language. Ahtna elder Sanford Nicolai best summed it up when he said at a potlatch in December of 1977:

> All this time for thousands of years, Indians look up at that mountain and call it K'elt'aeni. For hundreds of generations our forefathers look up and say K'elt'aeni. But Indians not very smart. First White Man come along, he look up and say, Ah ha, Mount Sanford, and he write it down on a map . . . and Mount Sanford it is today, my people.

Times are changing rapidly and negatively for our people. We are losing our heritage with every television set and radio that is turned on. Every commercial we watch or hear tells us that we should become something else, that we should want something else. Our young people leave our villages to find that something else. And everything we watch, read, or hear is in English. Today our language has fewer than twenty speakers, all very old, and there is little interest among our youth and young adults to revive it.

We recognize these losses. We are surrounded by them. While some efforts have been made to rekindle our ways, perhaps this collection provides the best set of examples. Our traditional stories, like those of any culture, do much more than simply relate mytho-historic events or tell fantastic acts of heroism and creation. Traditionally, these same narratives were told to youth to teach them—a kind of cultural primer. While the stories themselves have meaning and significance, so too does the actual telling; for it is from storytelling by family members that young listeners became captivated enough to learn the lesson, while at the same time, and perhaps more importantly, they also learn the language. Adult listeners also benefit from the stories, finding new and deeper meanings as they age and gain life experience.

This collection uses Ahtna words (mostly central dialect) throughout its pages so that its readers, Ahtna or not, might briefly be introduced to our language and its beauty and intricacies, and in doing so, stave off its extinction a while longer; because, as my late friend and linguistic mentor, Ken Hale, put it: "the loss of a language is part of the more general loss being suffered by the world, the loss of diversity of all things."

This collection is not the product of a single individual's work. These are the stories of a People, passed down for generations so that our children may know the natural world around them and at the same time learn to keep our Indian heritage alive by passing them on to future generations. It is a sad fact that most of our tribal members born after the 1950s don't even know these stories. But traditions have a way of being revived in the face of renewed interest when imminent loss becomes all too clear.

Although the author ultimately assembled and edited this volume, individual stories and variations were retold by members of the Ahtna Tribe from villages in the Copper River region, and some are borrowed with permission from *Atna' Yanida'a* (Kari, Billum and Buck, 1979) and *Indian Stories* (Tansy and Kari, 1982, reprinted in 1997), both of which are out-of-print. It is important to note that stories such as these are often considered property of specific clans; and as such are to be retold only by members of specific clans. This is somewhat true within Ahtna society as it is among other Alaska Native tribes. But there is a danger in restricting storytelling among clans. My father's clan is Taltsiine (Talcheena: "Comes from the sea"). Sadly, there are very few remaining Taltsiine Clan members left. Should those stories considered property of Taltsiine be allowed to disappear forever when the last clan member retells a myth for the very last time? Should the stories of any People suffer such a fate? A collection such as this may well outlast those who told them, to become—perhaps—the only lasting record of our storytelling tradition.

Because these stories are often told by different members within a clan, or even within the tribe, and because they are told at different times, there are often differences in the retellings. These variations are part of the tradition. Indeed, as tribal members mature, certain parts of a story may become more significant to them and, therefore, they focus more upon that significance than one might otherwise. For example, at Joe Goodlataw's (Chief Goodlataw's brother) potlatch, I was reminded that some of these versions differ from what someone from another village or clan might have heard when they were growing up. I recall how at a potlatch many years ago, I was dancing in full regalia when a young man in his late teens danced his way toward me, coming ever closer. He leaned in and spoke to me above the din of drumming, singing, and stomping feet. "You didn't write that one story the way my grandmother told it," he said. Of course, he was right. Oral stories, though revered, vary by storyteller. But I have tried diligently to maintain the general character of these stories after hearing numerous accounts by numerous elders from numerous villages.

This project was originally funded and supported by Ahtna, Inc., our federally-recognized Native Corporation, by the Ahtna Heritage Foundation Board of Directors, and by a distinguished committee of Ahtna elders who recommended other elders for personal interviews during this project, as well as for other important language projects. It began in the mid 1990s. The Ahtna People wanted to safeguard their stories, so I began a two-year project to interview every living elder who had stories to share. I visited elders from all eight villages and even at homes in Fairbanks or Anchorage. I became the living repository of our stories (and our language). The product of those interviews was the publication of *In the Shadows of Mountains*, which was so popular that the entire print run of two thousand copies was snatched up within months by tribal members. I remember I couldn't keep them on the table at our 1997 Annual Meeting. People grabbed them up ten at a time, some for themselves, others for relatives not present. For the most part, the book was never made available to the public or to libraries.

Then a curious thing happened.

Bolstered by the success of the book, elders who had not participated in the project came forward to offer their stories. I also found some of my old handwritten field notes from the 1980s where I had interviewed now-deceased elders such as Walter Charley and Sanford Nicolai. Nine new stories have been added to this collection and the name has been changed to more accurately reflect the contents. Also, a bibliography has been added for those who may be interested in such things. These stories deserve to be read and shared and remembered.

Ahtna is a small tribe. There are not many of us. But if you are to know us, as my friend Gary Snyder says, it will be in part through stories such as these.

This collection could not have been made possible without the support of the following organizations and individuals:

Ahtna, Inc.
Ahtna Heritage Foundation
Roy Ewan
Nicholas Jackson
Veronica Nicholas
Carolyn Craig
Donald Johns
Eileen Ewan
Cecilia Larson
Susan Larson
Lucille Brenwick
Ben Neeley
Mary Joe Smelcer
Herbert Smelcer
Morrie Secondchief
Joe Secondchief
Louise Tansy Mayo
Jake Tansy
Fred Stickwan

Johnny Goodlataw
John Billum
Molly Billum
Fred Ewan
Fred Sinyon
Millie Buck
Markle Pete
Harry Johns
Ruth Johns
Johnny Shaginoff
Larry Vienneau
James Kari
Gary Snyder
Barre Toelken
Alan Dundes
Jack Zipes
Katie John
Walter Charley

Special thanks to Bridget Donnelly, Bard Young, Dale Seeds, Amber Johnson, and Betsy and Neal Delmonico.

An Ahtna woman dips for salmon in the dangerously swift waters of the Copper River. Photo circa 1910.

Trickster:

Myths from the Ahtna Indians of Alaska

The Box of Water

*This story was told to me many years ago by Walter Charley, an impor-
tant traditional Ahtna culture bearer who was related to me and after whom
we named our tribe's college scholarship. Not surprisingly, variations of the
story exist in the mythology of neighboring coastal cultures such as Tlingit
and Eyak. In the past, Ahtna had occasional contact with Tlingit and Eyak,
especially for trading and occasional warfare.*

In the time long ago, when animals could speak and people had not
yet been created, Raven ruled the world. Back then Raven was as white
as snow. He was not black like he is now. One day Raven saw a stranger
standing on the shore while he was flying along the sea. He landed and
spoke to him.

"Who are you?" he asked. "I have never seen you before."

"I am Ganook," replied the stranger.

"Where did you come from?" asked Raven.

"I have always been here, without beginning or end," said Ganook.
"How long have you been living?"

Raven was intrigued.

"I have been alive since before the world stood in its place," boasted
the white Raven.

Then Raven asked Ganook how old he was, thinking surely he was
not as old as he.

"I was born before the seas came up from below," answered Ganook.

"You are older than I," conceded the astonished Raven.

Suddenly, Ganook took off his hat, and instantly a dense and men-
acing fog settled on the surface of the sea. It was so thick that Raven
could not see before him. He became scared and begged Ganook to

make the fog disappear. Ganook had done this to prove that he was more powerful.

Thereafter, Ganook invited his white feathered brother to join him at his great house for a feast. Inside the house was a large stone box with a lid upon which Ganook slept at night. Inside was the only fresh water in the world. Ganook shared some with Raven, but the greedy bird could not get enough of it because it tasted so good. He was used to drinking only sea water. After the feast, Raven began to tell stories of his adventures. He told many tales, and soon Ganook fell asleep on the stone box lid.

The deceitful Raven, ever the trickster, thought quickly and decided to steal some of the fresh water. He tricked Ganook by placing excrement beneath him and then awoke him saying how he had messed himself.

"Just look at yourself!" Raven exclaimed, laughing.

Ganook rushed out into the sea to bathe, and while he was away Raven quickly removed the heavy lid and drank some of the sweet water. But before he could escape, Ganook returned and saw what Raven was doing. He was angry that he had been so easily deceived. He grabbed Raven by the neck and began roasting him over a fire. The smoke turned Raven black.

Finally, Ganook released Raven, who flew away with some water still in his beak. As he flew, water dripping from his beak fell on the ground, forming the first rivers, streams, lakes, and ponds.

Walter Charley

Raven Steals the Stars, the Moon, and the Sun

Just as western religion suggests that the world was void of light in the very beginning, so too was the Ahtna world before Raven stole the sun, the moon, and the stars and released them. There are ethnographic accounts of this narrative in almost all Alaska Native mythologies. In some versions Raven turns himself into a hemlock needle to impregnate the young woman, while in others he becomes a spruce needle, a small fish, and even a piece of fine moss. Recorded as early as 1850 in Sitka by Heinrich J. Homberg, this version was told to me by my 80 year old, full-blood Ahtna grandmother, Mary Joe Smelcer, daughter of Tazlina Joe and granddaughter of Old Man Lake.

My mother told me this story about Raven. Not the black bird we see today. This Raven was like a god. He was the most powerful of all beings. He had made the animals, fish, trees, even the mountains and waters. He had made all living creatures, but they were all living in darkness because he had not made na'aay, the sun.

One day Raven learned that there was a great chief living along the banks of a distant river who had the sun, the moon, and the stars in three carved boxes. The great chief also had a very beautiful daughter. Both the princess and the treasures were well guarded.

This Raven, Saghani Ggaay, knew that he must trick the chief in order to steal his treasure, so he decided to turn himself into a grandchild of the great chief. He flew upon a tall tree near their house and waited. When the princess came to a small pond to get water, Raven turned himself into a small speck. Thus disguised, he fell into the girl's drinking cup. When she drank the water, she also drank the speck which was really Raven. Inside the chief's daughter, Raven became a baby and soon the young woman bore a son who was so dearly loved by the chief that he gave him whatever he asked for. But because the princess had no husband, the family had to hide the baby. And what a different baby it was. In no time at all it was grown and could speak.

The stars, the moon, and the sun were held in three very beautiful and ornately carved wooden boxes which sat on the dirt floor of the house. The one grandchild who was actually the Raven, wanted to play with the stars and the moon and wouldn't stop his crying until the grandfather gave them to him. As soon as he had them, though, Raven threw them up through the smoke-hole. Instantly, they scattered across the sky. Although the grandfather was unhappy, he loved his grandson too much to punish him for what he had done.

Now that he had tossed the stars and the moon out the smoke hole, the little grandson began crying for the box containing the sun. He cried and cried and would not stop. He was actually making himself sick because he was crying so much. Finally, the grandfather gave him the box and Raven played with it for a long time. Suddenly, though, he turned himself back into a bird and flew up through the smoke-hole with the box.

Once he was far away from the small village, Raven heard people speaking in the darkness and approached them.

"Who are you and would you like to have light?" he asked those people who lived in the dark.

Mary Joe Smelcer

They said that he was a liar; that no one could give light.

To show them that he was telling the truth, Raven opened the ornately carved box and let sunlight into the world. The people were so frightened by it that they fled to every corner of the world. This is why there are Raven's people everywhere.

　　Now there are stars, the moon, and the sun and it is no longer dark all the time.

na'aay　(naw-eye) "sun, moon" [used in the naming of months]

Saghani Ggaay　(sa-gaw-nee guy) "Little Trickster Raven"

How Raven Killed the Whale

Although Ahtna's traditional territory does not border the sea (though it comes close), this story is still part of our narrative literature. It also appears in the oral history of several other southeast Alaska Native Peoples. Interesting, my father's clan is Taltsiine (Talcheena), which means "comes from the sea." Perhaps this story, like others, first came to Ahtna country via migrations of families and clans from other regions. This version was told by Fred Sinyon to a group of youth at Culture Camp in 1996 while sitting around the campfire one evening.

As usual, Saghani Ggaay, Trickster Raven, was hungry. He had heard of a large whale near an island and so he went to see it for himself. The people in the nearby village were afraid of it. They were so afraid that they would not take their boats out to fish.

Raven flew to the place and carefully watched the whale, all the time thinking how he could trick it so that he could eat it. That smart bird knew that he would have lots to eat if he could kill the whale. Finally, an idea came to him. He flew into the forest and gathered dry wood which he tied to a pack on his back. Then Raven flew out across the water to a rock near the whale.

"Come close, Cousin Whale, so that I may speak with you," requested the sly bird.

Tełaani heard the sound and opened his eyes. He had been resting in the sunshine. When he saw the small bird who was speaking to him, Whale swam closer to the rock to speak. You see, animals could speak to each other back then.

"What do you want?" asked the whale whose rest was interrupted by the bird.

"I have come to tell you that we are cousins," Raven said.

"That is impossible. You are a puny bird and I am a whale. We are not cousins," replied Whale.

"It is true. We are cousins," said Raven. "I can prove it."

Tełaani was curious, so he asked Saghani Ggaay to prove their relation.

"If you will open your mouth," said Raven, "you will see how our throats are the same shape, which proves that we are cousins."

As Raven spoke, he opened his mouth to let the whale see his tiny throat.

Although the giant Killer Whale did not believe that they had anything in common, he slowly opened his mouth with its many teeth. When his mouth was opened just far enough, Raven quickly ran into his mouth and down his long throat. He was still wearing his bundle of dry wood, which he now used to build him a small fire. He cut slices of meat from inside the whale and began to cook it over the fire.

Whale knew that he had been tricked. He begged Raven not to eat his heart, this way he would stay alive. Raven agreed and spent many days inside the whale eating whenever he was hungry, which was most of the time.

After most of the meat was cooked and eaten, Raven began to think about getting out of the whale. One day, Whale told Raven that they were in shallow water and near land. Raven saw this as his chance to get out. He took his knife and cut out the whale's heart, and the poor whale died. After a short time the waves pushed Tełaani's great body onto a pebble beach. Raven cut a hole in the side of the water just big

Fred Sinyon tells stories at Culture Camp

enough to squeeze through and then he walked into the sunshine and flew high into the air, looking around for something else to eat.

Saghani Ggaay (sa-gaw-nee guy) "Little Trickster Raven"

Tełaani (te-klaw-nee) "Whale"

Zara Smelcer in traditional dress at Culture Camp

Raven and Loon: The Necklace Story

This particular version of a popular Ahtna myth is one of my favorites as it was told to me in Mendeltna by my grandmothers, Mary Joe Smelcer and her older sister Morrie Secondchief. There was a magical quality to the telling as both women recalled the story from their youth and took turns telling segments and seeking affirmation from the other. Versions of this narrative can be found in the mythologies of other Alaska Native cultures, including Eyak, which is a neighbor of Ahtna. Ruth Johns of Copper Center later told me a slightly different version.

In the time very long ago, when animals could speak and people had not yet been created, Raven and Loon were good friends and visited with one another often. Back in those days both birds were white. They were white all over. One day, Raven was flying around looking for food when he saw Loon—Dadzeni—swimming on a lake. He landed and asked his friend to come and visit him. The other bird swam to shore to talk with his friend.

"Let's paint each other," said the white Raven.

They looked around and found some black mud along the lake's edge, and with it Raven began to paint the white Loon's back and feathers black with white speckles, and then he made a pretty necklace around Loon's neck, his uk'os.

"You look so wonderful!" exclaimed Raven when finished.

Dadzeni looked at himself in the smooth lake's reflection and saw how pretty he was and that he had a beautiful necklace. But his head and chest was still white.

13

Raven asked his friend, "Please, paint me just as I have painted you so that I will look as pretty."

Loon took some mud and began painting. But Loon was not as good as Raven and he could not make him as pretty. Even though he tried very hard, he could not paint as well as his friend.

When he was done Raven looked at himself and saw that he was all black. Every part of him was black, even his feet, head, and beak were black. He did not even have a necklace around his neck. He began to jump up and down yelling at Loon.

My great aunt Morrie Secondchief at Tazlina

"Look at me! Look at me!" he screamed. "I am all black. You did not paint me like I painted you. I do not even have a pretty necklace!"

The angry Raven chased Loon all over trying to get him. He chased that Loon around that lake all day long. All that time the loon was saying that he was sorry.

Finally, Loon flew out to the middle of the lake where his angry friend could not get him. You see, Ravens can't swim. Raven stood on the beach and shouted at him. Then he picked up a handful of mud and threw it very far and hit Loon right on the head! He got him on the head. When he was tired of yelling, Raven flew away and they have not been friends again.

Ruth Johns of Copper Center tells stories

Since that time, Raven has been black all over and Loon has a black head and a pretty necklace.

Dadzeni (dad-zee-nee) "Loon"

uk'os (oo-kos) "neck"

The Mouse Story

I have encountered similar retellings of this story in neighboring Atha-baskan tribes' oral traditions, especially in Dena'ina (sometimes spelled Tana-ina). This story was also told to me years ago by the late Walter Charley.

Long ago, in a small village, there lived a young man. The people of the village worked very hard all summer putting away food for the long winter. They caught salmon with long dip nets, and they used fish traps to catch other fish, too. They worked like this preparing for winter.

One day this man was walking around looking for berries. In the brush beside him he saw a small mouse—dluuni—carrying a large fish egg—k'uun'—in its mouth. The mouse was struggling very hard to cross a log in its path.

The man saw this and helped the mouse. He gently lifted it over the log and placed it on the other side. The mouse quickly ran into the brush and was gone.

Winter came too early that year. It was cold and there wasn't enough food to put away. Half way through winter the food began to run out and the people became weak and sick. Surely they would not survive the winter.

One day, while the young man was out looking for anything to eat, he came upon a small house. Smoke was coming from its smoke hole. It was a very small house.

The young man heard a voice coming from inside which told him to turn around three times with his eyes closed. The man did this and became small enough to go through the tiny door—hwdatnetaani. Inside stood a man in a brown fur coat.

"We were expecting you. Come in. Sit down," he said.

17

The young man sat down and listened.

"Your people have no food. It is a very hard winter for them. But I will help you," said the strange man.

The man brought out a small pack which he began to fill with berries and fish meat and grease. He gave it to the young Indian man from the

The Man Who Married an Otter Woman

There are many transformation myths in which humans marry animals, who conceal their identity until the end of the story. There are numerous stories of bears marrying Indian women. This one was told to me by my great uncle Joe Secondchief during a visit to his cabin in Mendeltna. His wife, my great aunt Morrie Secondchief, translated the story from our Western dialect.

A young hunter saw some fresh land otter tracks in the snow leading to a little slough off a lake. We call them land otters tahwt'aey. The slough was mostly frozen, but the middle was still open. There were lots of tracks leading in and out of the water. That hunter crouched behind a tree stump and waited. Finally, that otter came swimming along and climbed out onto the ice looking for food. It was sleek, and its brown fur was the most perfect fur the hunter had ever seen. He stood up slowly and pulled back the string to his bow. The startled otter heard the sound and turned to see what it was. Seeing that it was about to be killed, the otter's black eyes welled up with tears. The hunter was just about to shoot when he saw how sad it seemed. He carefully let off on the bowstring and smiled at the otter.

"You are too sad and beautiful to kill," he said. "Go now, and live in peace."

Hearing that, the land otter slid back into the water and swam away, stopping once to look back at the man.

Maybe you think that's the end of the story, but it's not.

The next summer, that young hunter, who was a chief's son, was busy building a salmon drying rack, called a daxi, near where the Tazlina River goes into the Copper River when a beautiful young woman walked out from the woods. She was tall and thin, and she had long dark hair and beautiful dark eyes. She was the most beautiful woman he had ever seen. The mysterious woman helped the young man finish building the daxi and then he took her back to his village to meet his people.

Everyone kept asking her where she came from, but she just answered by pointing eastward and saying in her queer way that seemed ancient, "My village is in that direction, beside a lake at the base of a mountain."

The hunter and the woman were soon married and she quickly became pregnant. They lived in his village all summer, catching and drying salmon. But one day during fall, at the time when geese fly south, she asked to go visit her people back in her old village. The husband agreed. He was curious to meet her family. After several days of walking they arrived at the lake where the young man had gone hunting, the lake where he had seen the land otter on the ice. But there was no village along the banks.

"Why have you brought me here?" he asked. "There is no one living here."

The wife took off her clothes and her moose-hide moccasins.

"I am the last of the Land Otter People living on this lake," she said, standing naked before her husband. "Indians have hunted all the others, including my parents and my brothers and sisters. I came in search of a husband so we can populate the lake with our children and grandchildren. Last winter you spared my life because I was sad and beautiful. I left the lake to search for you."

Having said that she dove into the water. When she emerged she was an otter, the same one the hunter had let live that winter day. She floated effortlessly just off shore, anxiously waiting. The young hunter stood on the shore looking at the otter woman and then back toward where his village was. Finally, he set down his bow and arrows, took off his clothes, and dove into the lake and also emerged as an otter. He jumped in because he loved her so much.

tahwt'aey (tawt-kay) "land otter" (Lutra canadensis)

daxi (daw-kee) "free-standing salmon drying rack made from poles"

John Smelcer and his great aunt and uncle, Morrie and Joe
Secondchief

When Raven Was Killed

My grandmother, Mary Joe Smelcer told me this unique story several years ago. I have not encountered a similar version of this particular narrative anywhere, which does not imply that other versions don't exist—only that I have not found them.

Long ago, way back in the time when animals spoke, there was this Raven. This wasn't the same raven you see flying around nowadays. He was magical, powerful – both creator and destroyer. We call him Saghani Ggaay, "Little Trickster Raven."

Well, Saghani Ggaay had played so many tricks on mankind for so long that one day a chief—kaskae—decided to kill him. The chief invited Raven to visit him at his village. When the black bird wasn't paying attention, the chief threw a skin bag over Raven and tied it tightly shut so that the troublesome bird could not escape.

With the heavy pack on his back, the man began to climb a very steep and high mountain. We say dghelaay in Ahtna. It was very dark inside the bag, and Raven could not see. He asked the man what he was doing, but the chief ignored him.

As the man climbed higher, Raven spoke out again.

"Where are you taking me?" he asked.

The chief just kept on climbing.

"I can tell that you are climbing a high mountain," insisted Raven. "Why are you carrying me there? What are you going to do to me?" Raven was worried.

The man ignored him still and continued to climb.

Raven warned the chief that he would be sorry if he killed him, saying that bad things would befall his clan.

When the chief was on top of the mountain, he threw the skin bag with Raven inside over the steep side. As it fell, it struck the cliff and ripped open. Raven was torn to pieces by the jagged rocks as he crashed to the ground below. The chief had killed Raven!

When the chief returned to his village, he showed his people the pieces of Saghani Ggaay so that they would know what he had done. All the villagers called him a great chief for killing the mischievous trickster. For several days the village celebrated.

Finally, though, some people began to notice that all of the water was gone. They went to the river, but it was dry. They went to a lake, and it too was empty. There was no water to be found anywhere!

The people began to become thirsty. They knew that they could not live long without water. One day, they asked a shaman why the water had vanished. The shaman told them that it was because the chief had killed Raven. Now the villagers were not happy that Raven was dead. They wanted him back before everyone died.

The shaman told the chief that he had to put Raven's pieces back together again. When he had done this, Raven jumped instantly to life again! He hopped up and down and started to fly away. But then he stopped and asked the chief why he had been brought back to life.

"All of the water has gone," he replied. "Only you can return it."

Raven flew up into the air, higher and higher, and then he spoke down to the man.

"Look around you, there is water everywhere."

The villagers turned towards the river and lake and saw that they were filled with water again.

As Raven flew into the distance, the chief yelled to him, "We will never try to kill you again!"

To this day, because of that promise, Indians do not hunt or kill ravens.

Saghani Ggaay (sa-gaw-nee guy) "Trickster Raven in *yanida'a* (long ago) stories"

kaskae (kask-a) "chief, wealthy man"

dghelaay (ga-lie) "mountain"

How Porcupine Got Quills

Similar versions of this origin myth occur in many of the eleven Athabaskan tribes of Alaska. Indeed, in the oral histories of almost all indigenous peoples of the world there are origin myths explaining how things, especially animals, came to be.

When Porcupine—Nuuni—was first created by Raven, he had soft hair. He didn't have the sharp quills he now has. Because Nuuni had no means to protect himself, he was always being teased by other animals, especially by Bear and Wolf who bothered him the most. They would take his food away and leave him hungry, or they would harass him just for the fun of it.

It happened that way for a long time until poor Porcupine learned a few ways to escape from Tsaani's and Tikaani's tauntings. His best trick was to climb a tree where neither Bear nor Wolf could reach him. But sometimes there was not a tall enough or strong enough tree nearby, so Tsaani and Tikaani would steal his food again. Also, Nuuni was too slow to run away from his enemies. He was really having a rough time of it!

One summer day, while Bear and Wolf were teasing him, they shoved him into a hole full of mud. When Porcupine came out of the hole his soft hair was covered with mud. Tsaani and Tikaani laughed at him and ran away with his food again.

Since there was no river nearby and because it was such a hot summer day, Nuuni's hair soon dried, becoming very stiff and brittle.

The next day Bear saw Porcupine walking down a trail. When he came over to push him down as he always did, he was quite surprised when his paws touched Porcupine's hair. Bear roared in pain and ran away.

From that time on, Bear and Wolf never bothered Nuuni again, and all porcupines have sharp quills, called q'ok, so that bigger animals cannot hurt them or take away their food as they easily used to do.

Nuuni (new-nee) "Porcupine"

Tsaani (chaw-nee) "Grizzly Bear"

Tikaani (tik-a-nee) "Wolf"

q'ok (kee-awk) "quills" [pronounced as one syllable]

When Raven Killed
Grizzly Bear

This story is a variation of many stories cataloging Raven's trickery in killing his fellow beings to eat them. In a Tlingit story he runs down the throat of a whale into his belly and eats him from the inside out (See page 9 for Fred Sinyon's version.). In an Iñupiaq variation, he tricks an entire village, killing them in an avalanche and dining on their eyeballs and feasting on their corpses all spring. This story was told to me by Johnny Goodlataw of Tazlina Village while I helped him put his fishwheel into the Copper River. I had received a special permit from the State of Alaska to allow us to start fishing a week earlier than anyone else as part of an Indian youth education program I was directing called Positive Pathways.

One day in the springtime, when there was still plenty of snow on the hills and mountains, Raven was searching for something to eat. He was always hungry, that Raven. He was flying around when he saw Grizzly Bear looking for food on a hillside. Raven had a wicked idea, so he flew down to talk.

"Do you want to have some fun?" he asked with a sly smile.

"What shall we do?" replied Grizzly Bear.

"Let's slide on the snow."

Raven went first. He slid on his back down a snowy slope. When he was at the bottom he stood up and shouted to Grizzly Bear.

"That was fun! It's your turn!"

So Grizzly Bear slid down the slope on his haunches. After that Raven saw an even higher and steeper slope.

"Let's slide down that one," he said, pointing a black wing.

But Grizzly Bear thought it looked too steep.

"I don't know. That looks pretty dangerous," he said.

To show him that it was safe to slide on, Raven flew up to the top and slid down on his back again. He went really fast and he spun around a few times, but he made it safely to the bottom.

"That was great fun!" he shouted up to Grizzly Bear who was standing at the top, anxiously peering down the slope.

But Grizzly Bear was unsure. He kept pacing back and forth, huffing and snorting, stopping every now and then to look over the edge. While Grizzly was nervously pacing, Raven made a sharp spear using his knife. He set the angled spear firmly into the packed snow at the bottom of the snowy slide so that it would impale the bear when he came down. But the hesitant bear wouldn't slide down.

"If I made it, you can make it!" Raven jeered. "You're so much bigger and stronger than I am."

Finally, goaded by Raven's taunting, Grizzly Bear decided to slide down. He went faster and faster down the slope. He went so fast that the spear planted at the bottom of the hill went right through his heart and killed him. Even though bears are pretty skinny when they first come out of their dens in the spring, Raven ate him anyhow.

Johnny Goodlataw and his fishwheel at the Wrangell St. Elias National Park Tourist Center

The Blind Man and the Loon

The story of The Blind Man and the Loon is perhaps one of the most common of Alaska Native myths, second only to Raven Steals the Sun, Stars, and the Moon. Accounts of this story appear in Yupik, Inupiaq, Upper Tanana, Tanaina, Eyak, and Ahtna ethnography. Because Eyak is a neighboring tribe, and because Ahtna historically traded with them, it is no wonder that their versions are so similar. Like many narratives, it teaches a moral lesson: "Don't be greedy and be kind to those less fortunate." Johnny Shaginoff told me this story.

A husband and wife once lived inland along the Copper River. The husband was blind, and so the wife had to work hard to gather enough food for them. Because the man was blind, the two had not had any game meat for a long time. One day, though, the wife saw a large moose walking by.

"Deniigi is walking by," she whispered.

"Quick," said the husband, "hand me my bow and arrows."

The wife gave them to him. Because she was not strong enough to draw back the bowstring, she had to let the husband shoot. But because he could not see, the wife had to guide his aim.

"Is that good?" he asked her. "Am I aiming at the moose?"

"Yes," she replied. "You are aiming correctly."

The blind man let loose the arrow and instantly he heard the unmistakable sound of the arrow striking the animal's side. The heavy moose lurched forward and then fell down dead.

The wife did not tell her husband the truth. Instead, she had a plan.

33

"Quick, husband," she said, "it is running away. Shoot again."
The wife helped him aim again. But this time the arrow hit the ground because there was no moose where she had pointed him. She lied to him saying how poorly he had shot.

"You missed it! It got away," she said insultingly.

She told him to stand where he was while she gathered the two arrows. The wife pulled the bloody arrow from the moose's side and wiped it clean in the grass. Then she stuck it in the mud along the riverbank and took it back to her blind husband.

He smelled the tip. "It smells like blood," he told her.

"No," she replied. "You only hit the mud. You did not kill the moose."

She took her husband back to their camp near a small lake behind the river. Then she went back to cut off pieces of the moose for herself. She was not going to tell him the truth. She was going to eat all of the meat and not share any with him.

This went on for days, her eating the meat by herself, until one day the blind man heard a voice coming from the lake.

"Come here," it said.

This startled the man because he did not know anyone was there.

He stood and answered the voice, "I am blind, I cannot see."

The voice replied, "Come here. You can feel your way."

The man cautiously found his way to the lake's edge. It was a giant loon who spoke to him. It spoke again.

"Sit down on my back and hold on to my neck feathers."

The blind man did as he said and Loon—Dadzeni—dove under the water with him and swam around the lake twice. When he came up for air, the loon spoke to him.

"Now, look around," it said.

The man opened his eyes."

"I can see a little," he said excitedly.

"Close your eyes again and hold your breath," demanded the loon.

The two dove under the water again and swam around the lake once more. This time when the loon came up the blind man could see perfectly! He thanked the magical bird, promised never to hunt his relatives, and walked back to find his wife to tell her the good news. When he found her he saw that she was boiling some meat and he saw the dead moose that he had killed in the bushes nearby. She had lied to him and now she was not even going to share the food with him. This made him very angry.

When the wife saw him she nervously said, "I was just cooking some meat for you."

The husband was so mad because she had tricked him that he shoved her head into the boiling pot and killed her.

From then on he always had good luck and was a great hunter.

Deniigi (den-nee-gee) "Moose"

Dadzeni (dad-zee-nee) "Loon"

Fox and the Greedy Wolverine

This story, first recorded by John Billum in Atna' Yanida'a, *is very similar to one told in Tlingit oral history. In the Tlingit version, though, the characters are human, and a greedy young daughter-in-law turns into an owl as her punishment. Fox's name in this story, Ciił Hwyaa, is not the literal translation for the animal. Instead, it is a nickname for this mythic character often used in Ahtna storytelling.*

A very long time ago, in *yanida'a*, Fox was married and had several children. They all lived in the woods where they hunted for food. But things had not been good for Ciił Hwyaa lately. Fox had not brought any meat home in a while even though he hunted all the time.

During this hungry time, Wolverine—Nałtsiis—came to visit. He asked Fox if he could marry one of his daughters. Fox and his wife thought about this and they agreed to give her to him. Because they didn't have enough meat, they gave her away thinking that at least Wolverine would feed her.

One day Wolverine went out hunting. After a time he returned to the village with two beavers. Everyone was happy. Now they would all eat well. Wolverine skinned the beavers and began to cook the meat. His new mother-in-law came and asked for a piece of meat. She thought surely her new son-in-law would share with his new family. But that greedy Nałtsiis did not intend to share any of his meat. Instead, he threw a piece of old, dried up moose leg bone at her.

"Here. Cook that!" he said to his wife's mother.

The mother-in-law ran home to tell her husband what had happened.

Fox agreed that she had been treated badly, but told her that she should ask again tomorrow.

The next day Wolverine again insulted his mother-in-law.

And the day after that he did the same thing. That greedy Wolverine didn't share any of his meat—not even with his wife. Fox and his wife were very angry. They had given their daughter to Wolverine thinking that he would at least provide for her and act properly towards his in-laws.

The following evening Fox went hunting and he saw moose tracks. He followed the tracks in the fresh snow until he saw that Wolverine was hunting Deniigi, too. From a hill he watched as Nałtsiis chased the moose and then quickly grew tired and let it escape.

On his way back to the village he passed Fox and told him how he had almost caught a moose, how he wrestled with it, but it got away. Fox said that he would kill it.

"You are too small to kill it," laughed the Wolverine.

But after they parted, Fox went to where the moose was and he killed it. He skinned it and took some of the meat home to his family, who were all hungry by now. After they had eaten he moved his whole family, including his married daughter, to a camp near the moose.

Wolverine was out hunting by himself, so he did know what had happened. At the moose camp they had enough meat for a long time.

When Wolverine finally found them at the camp, he was invited to eat, too. He ate and ate and ate until he was very full. He was so full that he grew tired and soon fell asleep. While he was asleep, Fox cooked a lot of fat. Then he carefully crept over to that place where Nałtsiis was sleeping and he poured the burning hot grease all over Wolverine and killed him. He did this because Wolverine had been so selfish and greedy.

Yanida'a (yan-i-da-a) "mythic times/long ago story time"

Ciił Hwyaa (keeth who-yah) "Fox in yanida'a; smart man"

Nałtsiis (natch-cheese) "Wolverine"

Deniigi (den-nee-gee) "Moose" [bulls only]

The Doc Billum Family

How Wolverine Became Fierce

Despite their size—an average male weighs 50-60 pounds—wolverines (Gulo gulo, Latin for "glutton") are so ferocious that even grizzly bears avoid tangling with them. There's even an account of a wolverine killing a 1,000-pound polar bear by clinging to its throat until the bear suffocated. Reclusive by nature, wolverines are rarely seen in the wild. In his lifetime of hunting, fishing, and backpacking Alaska, the author has only seen one once. This version was told by Joe Secondchief, who had hunted and trapped in Ahtna Country all of his life.

A long time ago, Wolverine wasn't ferocious. He looked more like a big weasel than he does nowadays. He didn't have powerful bone-cracking jaws. He didn't have sharp claws, and his body wasn't built as thick and tough as it is today. Back then, everyone picked on Wolverine and took his food away from him. Even Porcupine and Beaver had fun pushing him around and making fun of him.

Poor Wolverine really had a tough time of it.

One day, Raven watched as Wolf took Wolverine's dead rabbit away from him. Then, after Wolverine found another rabbit a little later, Raven watched as Grizzly Bear took that rabbit away, too. Raven decided to have some fun. He transformed Wolverine, giving him his strong jaws full of sharp teeth. He made his body heavier and his hide thicker. He made his claws longer and sharper. He also gave him the meanest temperament of any animal. When he was done changing Wolverine, Raven laughed at the ferocious little creature he had made.

A few days later, Wolverine was eating a caribou carcass he had found when a pack of wolves came by and tried to take it from him. They were surprised when, instead of running away as usual, Wolverine turned on them savagely to defend his dinner. He was so terrifying that the wolves left in search of a safer meal to eat. A little later, Grizzly Bear came by and also tried to take Wolverine's meal away from him. They got into a scrap, and Wolverine, who didn't even weigh one-tenth of Grizzly Bear, was such a formidable foe that Grizzly Bear gave up and walked away, licking his wounds and looking over his shoulder wondering what had happened to the puny little Wolverine he had always known.

Since then, nobody ever messes with Wolverine.

Nobody.

Ever.

Copper River Indians, circa 1900

How Moose Got His Dewlap

Biologists are uncertain of the purpose of a bull moose's dewlap, the flap of skin that hangs under the chin (also called the bell). Some think it serves as a visual indicator of dominance, the way large antlers do. But the Ahtna, who have hunted moose for thousands of years, have their own idea. This story was told by Ruth Johns during the nightly campfire talk at Culture Camp in 1997. Surprisingly, there are few stories about moose.

One day Moose—Deniigi—was eating alder leaves along the gravel banks of the upper Klutina River, way up near Klutina Lake—Tl'atii Bene'. Back then Moose didn't have a dewlap like they do nowadays. He was walking along eating when Grizzly Bear jumped out from some dense brush and clamped his jaws around Moose's neck, trying to take him down. Moose tried to break loose, but Grizzly really had him by the neck. Grizzly pulled and pulled, tugged and tugged, trying to take down the large moose. But as the hungry bear pulled, the skin on Moose's neck began to stretch. It stretched longer and longer, thinner and thinner. Finally, Grizzly's teeth couldn't hold on to the neck-skin any longer. Moose broke free and escaped by jumping into the swift river and swimming to the other side. That's what Klutina means, "Swift River." Ever since then, moose have dewlaps to make it harder for bears and wolves to catch them that way.

Deniigi (dee-nee-gee) moose [bulls only]

Tl'atii Bene' (kloo-tee ben) "Klutina Lake"

Tazlina Lake Monster

Tazlina Lake Monster

My grandmother told me this story about a monster that lived in Tazlina Lake, which is formed from the meltwater of Tazlina Glacier. Grandmother was born and raised at Tazlina Lake Village, which was abandoned after The Great Death (more commonly known as the 1918-1920 Spanish Influenza epidemic) killed many of the villagers there.

Way long ago, back before there were white people in Ahtna country, there was a village at Tazlina Lake near Mendeltna Creek—Bendil Na'. When I was a little girl we lived there and we hunted sheep—debae—up in the mountains near the glacier. We had to walk there on a trail that went by the river for maybe twenty miles.

A long time ago hunters used to hunt caribou—udzih—and catch salmon at Tazlina Lake. There was lots of caribou around. There still is sometimes. There were big moose sometimes, too.

Once in a while I heard stories about a giant monster that lived in the lake. People said they saw it sometimes. The stories say that it was so big that it could catch and eat whole caribou swimming across parts of the lake. It would come up from underneath and pull them under water and eat them. Because of their fear of the gguux—monster—Ahtna men avoided the middle of the lake which was very deep and rough.

I remember one time when I was a little girl. I must have been six. My father, Tazlina Joe, your granddaddy, came home all out of breath and clearly frightened. He said that while he was out in his canoe looking for game along the lake edge, he suddenly saw a giant monster come swimming alongside his canoe. He said it was longer than his canoe and it had giant scales and a long head.[1]

---

[1] Sturgeon, which can grow to sixteen feet long, once migrated into Tazlina Lake following spawning salmon. I guess that could be what my grandfather saw.

Bendil Na' (ben-deel-na) "Mendeltna Creek"

debae (deb-a) "dall sheep"

udzih (you-jee) "caribou"

gguux (goo) "monster, or worm"

The Giant Ice Worm

Many of the stories I heard as a boy were while sitting around a camp-fire during hunting season or at fish camp. One of the fondest memories is of a moose hunt in the fall in the 1970s. My brother and I went hunting with my uncle Herbert, who was an important Native leader in Alaska. We were camping where we could see a glacier in the distance when Herb told this story. Imagine my surprise years later, when, while exploring glaciers throughout Alaska, I learned that there really are worms that live on the surface of glaciers, only they are very small and eat pollen blown onto the ice from surrounding hillsides.

They say that giant ice worms live in the glaciers. They make the holes (moulins) and ice caves you see in the glaciers. They say they are very long, maybe forty or fifty feet long. Maybe bigger. I don't know. I've never seen one. They come out of their holes to hunt caribou, moose, or sheep high up on the hills near the glacier. They also eat bears, especially when they go up high in the fall to eat blueberries and to look for fat marmots among the rocks. They say the creaking and cracking sounds are the worms moving around in the ice. I heard a story when I was young about some hunters that disappeared after trying to cross a glacier to hunt some sheep they saw on the other side of the valley. They say a giant ice worm must have got them.

Ahtna Group Photo

Fox and Wolf

This story, like Fox and Wolverine, also appeared in Atna' Yanida'a *as told by John Billum. This version, told to me in my youth, is slightly different from that account.*

Once, way back in story time, when animals spoke and there were no people in Copper River country, there was this fox who acted just like people. He was very smart and a good hunter. One day while he was out hunting, Fox came upon a track which he followed for a while. Soon he came upon a snare which someone had set to catch small animals. He kept following the tracks until he came upon an old woman Wolf—Tikaani—walking ahead of him.

Fox walked up to the old lady and spoke to her.

"Hello. I have not seen you before. Where are you from?"

The old woman replied, "Oh, I am from around here. What is your name?"

"I am Ciił Hwyaa," answered Fox.

The old lady Tikaani smiled as she spoke to him.

"Oh, you are a smart man." That is what she said.

"Yes," said Fox. "That is what my name means."

They spoke for a little while and then Fox left her. As he was walking along the trail ahead of her he came across another snare. He thought about a funny trick. He took off his clothes and stuffed them full of dried grass and moss so that it looked like him. Then he placed a large piece of fat—tlagh—on the breast. After he had done these things he placed it in the snare so that it looked as though he had been caught by the snare. Then he hid behind a tree and waited for the old woman to come along.

49

After a while the old lady came down the trail. She saw that her snare had caught the smart man and she ran up to it, smiling because she was so happy.

"You thought you were so smart. But I have caught you in my snare!" she said as she took out her skinning knife.

She took her knife and cut out the breast.

"Oh," she said. "Look how really fat it is." She was happy because meat with lots of fat is a good thing indeed. She cut some sticks nearby to roast the meat over a fire.

"This stick will be for my big brother, and this one is for my little brother." That is what she said while cutting them.

Now that she had her roasting sticks and a cooking fire, she took her knife and began to skin Fox. It didn't take long for her to learn that she had been tricked by that Fox.

"Oh! He is too smart for his own good," she said.

Hearing this, Ciił Hwyaa jumped out of his hiding place and laughed and laughed. He had really tricked her.

"Ha! Ha! You really thought you had me," laughed Fox.

The old lady Wolf became angry and ran after him. They ran through the mountains where there was snow on the ground. The younger and faster Fox was too fast for the old lady and soon she became tired. When night came she froze to death. Then Fox skinned her and took the meat back to the place where her snares were and he cooked the meat on her own roasting sticks.

Soon he heard sounds. Someone was coming. Fox hid behind a tree and waited. Then a whole family of wolves entered camp. They looked around and saw the meat cooking and saw that there was no one home. they thought this was their sister's camp, so they started to eat.

"This meat tastes like our sister," complained one of the wolves.

Just then Fox jumped out from his hiding place and began to laugh at the family of wolves.

"Ha! Ha! Ha! You ate your sister!"

The gray wolves ran after that Fox. They chased him back up to the mountains. Fox tried to roll a big rock down on them but he couldn't move it. Instead, he hid behind it with a heavy club and waited. When one of the brothers walked by he killed him with the stick. Then he killed another. After a while he had killed all but two of the wolves, who were too smart to go where their brothers had gone. They had become wise to Fox's tricks.

Tikaani (tik-aw-nee) "wolf"

Ciił Hwyaa (keeth who-yah) "smart man; nick-name for Fox"

tlagh (tlah) "fat, grease"

Hunting Camp of Upper Copper River

Stone Woman

Stone Woman

*Along the Glenn Highway, about half way between Anchorage and Glenn-
allen, overlooking the Matanuska Glacier, there is a mountain that rises
steeply from the valley and is unlike the mountains around it. I have climbed
it many times. There's even a cave where sheep wait out bad weather. Ahtna
Indians call it "Stone Woman Mountain" (its Ahtna name is Natsede'aayi)
and there is a story about its origin. My grandmother, Mary Joe Smelcer,
told me the story many years ago while we were driving by it, and Harry
Johns of Copper Center later retold it to me. Nowadays, there is a sign
posted by the Alaska Highway Department on the east side of the mountain
that retells the myth from this book.*

My father's family's clan is Talcheena Clan (while I am of the Indian
Paint Clan, tsisyu, because of our matrilineal system). In our language,
Talcheena means "came from the sea." It is said that long ago, before
things became the way they are now, that Ahtna came from another
place to settle this Copper River basin. This is the story of one woman
back when people first moved from the sea to this country.

It is said that some people decided to move from the sea into Indian
country, but to get there they would have to walk a long ways. They
would have to cross many mountains, rivers, and glaciers. It would be
very hard, especially for the very young and the very old.

To help them on their journey, Raven made the people become giants. They were much bigger than they are now. A hungry man could
eat a whole caribou—*udzih*— at one sitting. Raven's help made it easier
for the people to climb the rugged mountains and cross the swift waters and dangerous glaciers. He helped the people, but he made them
promise that they would not look back to where they came from; they
could only think about where they were going.

"If someone looks back, something terrible will happen." That is what he warned them.

Storyteller Harry Johns at Tazlina

The people began their long march and just before they crossed into the country where Ahtna people now live, one young woman who was carrying her baby—*sc'enggaay*—on her back in a baby basket (papoose) —*ts'aatl'*—began to think about her home. She thought of what she was leaving behind. Maybe she liked her old home and didn't want to leave it. She became so homesick that she turned to look back in the direction from where she had come, even though she had been told not to look back that way.

No sooner did she turn and look than she turned into stone. Because she was a giant, she became a giant rock. She turned into a mountain! That young mother became a mountain because she did not listen to what Raven had said to her and all those other Indians who were on that journey from the sea.

Today, people can still see her standing alone glacier and those mountains behind her. If you can still see her baby asleep on her back.

Tsisyu (shi-shu) "Indian Paint Clan"

udzih (you-jee) "caribou" [as in udzisyu: Caribo

sc'enggaay (sken-guy) "baby; infant"

ts'aatl' (chot-leh) "baby basket; papoose"

Bush Indians

Parents in many world cultures often warn their children that some boogey-man, gnome, fairy, or troll might take them away if they stray too far in the forest or go near forbidden places. They are invented to keep children from going near rivers, lakes, cliffs, or any place which may be dangerous to children. We have such creatures in our culture; we call them Bush Indians. Lucille Brenwick, born in Copper Center, related this account to me and Fred Sinyon told me a similar version.

When we were growing up back in the old days, our parents used to tell us that if we wandered too far away from camp, or went too near the river, Bush Indians would get us.

Bush Indians weren't just your normal Indians. They say that they were taller than a big man, and they were hairy all over. I guess they must have looked kind of like Bigfoot. Bush Indians lived like savages in the woods and they captured little children as slaves. They say that they would even eat them sometimes, too. Whenever our parents didn't want us to go near some place they would tell us to watch out for Bush Indians. We'd be so scared, especially at night, that we'd just stay right close to our family. We wouldn't go any-

Lucille Brenwick

where.

They say that a long time ago, a Bush Indian was wounded by Ahtna Indians. They say that he was hurt so bad that he later died after he got back to his people. He was buried up on the mountain, on Kełt'aeni—Mt. Wrangell—and that is why there is smoke coming from up there. It's his funeral flame burning.

Kełt'aeni (Kelth-taw-nee) "Mt. Wrangell" is a sometimes active volcano.

How Camprobber Got His Face

This story is very much like the Raven and Loon story in that it tells how certain animals came to be in the way they are (one of the primary purposes of myths). This narrative, though, involves Woodpecker and Camp-robber (common gray jay). This particular retelling was from my uncle, Herbert Smelcer, who was unable to recall where he had first heard it.

Back in yanida'a, when animals spoke and acted just like people, Camprobber— Stakalbaey—and Woodpecker—Cen'lkatl'i—were friends. At least, they were friends until this one day.

Back in those times, those long ago times, Camprobber was completely gray and Woodpecker had long tail feathers—*t'aa.* That is the way it was back then.

One day, though, Camprobber and Woodpecker were talking to each other. They were standing near a campfire and speaking about something. Then they began to argue about something. Woodpecker became so mad that he grabbed Camprobber and shoved his face into the fire He had ash all over his face!

Stakalbaey was very mad now, and as Woodpecker tried to fly away, he jumped up and grabbed his tail feathers. He held on until all of the feathers were pulled right out of that Woodpecker's tail!

Since that time, woodpeckers have no long tail feathers, and camp-robbers have spots on their face from the ash of the fire that Woodpecker pushed him into so long ago.

yanida'a (yan-i-da-a) "story time, mythic time"

Stakalbaey (stok-all-bay) "camprobber (gray jay)"

Cen'lkatl'i (ken-skaw-klee) "woodpecker"

t'aa (k-taw) "feathers [pronounced as one syllable]"

Herbert Smelcer

How Rabbit Got His Tail

This story is unique to Ahtna storytelling tradition. It is one of those wonderful stories that teaches us how things came to be; in this case how rabbits got their small, puffy tails just as another story taught us how porcupines got their quills. While most myths are not place-specific, that is they do not mention a specific location geographically, this one, like "When They Killed the Monkey People" does. A similar telling appears in Atna' Yanida'a *and in* Indian Stories. *The latter, a narrative from Cantwell, was retold by Jake Tansy, but Ruth Johns told me a similar version.*

A long time ago, an Indian from Tazlina Village went hunting along the Tazlina River near where it joins the Copper River. He hunted all day long until it became dark. Then he made a bed of spruce boughs to sleep on. The sound of nearby running water soon put him to sleep.

After the man was gone for several days, some of the other men went out to search for him. They followed the trail along the Tazlina River until they came to its confluence with the Copper. There they found the dead hunter. They didn't know why he was dead, only that he had a small, round hole in his neck.

After a while, the people in the village began to forget about the dead hunter, and another man went hunting alone in the same place. When he didn't return, the people searched for him and found him dead in the same way as the first man.

Because the two men had died so strangely, the villagers became scared. They did not know what had happened to the two hunters, but they knew they didn't want the same thing to happen to them! They were so frightened that they stopped hunting and they stayed very close to the village. Soon, though, their food supplies ran low. They even ran out of dried salmon. The people became hungry.

The problem became worse and worse until one smart man, Ciił Hwyaa, decided to find out what was happening. He left one early morning and followed the same trail as the two hunters. He followed that trail down the Tazlina to where it ran into the Copper River. When he came to the place they had died, Ciił Hwyaa built a small camp.

On the way he had seen nothing strange, certainly nothing to explain the men's deaths. But as he walked, he gathered large flat stones from along the river's edge. Since the hunters had small holes in their necks, he placed one flat stone against his neck and wrapped it with leather so that it could not be seen. He placed another stone under his clothes against his heart just in case. Once he had done these things, he pretended to go to sleep. He closed his eyes, but he was really awake. He was waiting for something to happen.

Soon, that smart man heard something in the woods. Something was coming down the trail and making a thumping sound. Ciił Hwyaa opened his eyes just a little and saw that it was only a rabbit—ggax— coming down the trail. The man lay quietly and waited for the rabbit. When it was close enough, the rabbit jumped into the air and landed on the man's neck with his sharp tail pointed downward.

You see, in the old times rabbits had sharply pointed tails which they used to protect themselves from other animals. But this mischievous rabbit had been using his tail to kill Indians while they were asleep.

When the rabbit came down on Ciił Hwyaa's neck, his sharp tail landed right on the flat stone. Ggax jumped high into the air and started screaming in pain. His tail was now all bent.

The hunter returned to his village and told the people what had happened. No one was ever killed by rabbits again, and since that time all rabbits have soft bent tails.

Ciił Hwyaa (keeth whoo-yah) "smart man; sometimes used for Fox"

ggax (gok) "rabbit" [as in the place name, Ggax Kuna', "Rabbit River"]

Chief Stickwan on the trail with family

Raven and Goose-Wife

Every fall many Alaskan birds, especially waterfowl and arctic terns, migrate south to warmer climates. One word for fall translated means, "That time when birds gather to go to that place." But Ravens don't migrate. Raven stays near his people. This story, retold to me by my grandmother Mary Joe Smelcer, also appears in neighboring Han and Tanana mythology.

It is said that Raven once fell in love with a beautiful young goose woman. They stayed together all summer until summer came to its end. Snow began to fall in the mountains and nights became colder. It was time to fly south; time for birds to gather to go to that place.

The goose girl loved Raven, but she wanted to fly south with her relatives. Raven decided to go with her because he loved her so much and because she would not stay with him in Atna' Nen'—Indian Country.

Now, Raven can fly as well as any bird, but he cannot fly for very long at one time. He cannot fly very far without rest. In this way he is like kuggaedi, the mosquito. He tried to keep up with his wife and her relatives, but he was always tired and falling far behind. When the geese—xax—did stop to rest and eat, they stopped at places where there was no food for Raven. Because of this, he was growing weaker and weaker every day.

The geese were in a hurry to get away from the snow and cold, and they did not like waiting for that slow Raven. His goose-wife let him ride on her back, but she couldn't carry him that way for long. The goose-girl's parents and brothers each took turns carrying Raven on their backs, too. They took turns like that until they came to the ocean.

The father-in-law told Raven that the ocean was very wide and that it was very hard to cross. He told him how there would be no place for him to rest. Goose-Wife's father and brothers said that they would no longer carry Raven on their backs.

Raven thought about this and decided that he would have to stay. He said good-bye to his beloved wife and then he flew back into the country where he has lived ever since. Now ravens are here all the time because they can't fly south across the ocean like geese.

Ahtna' Nen' (Ot-na Nen) "Ahtna land, Indian Country"

kuggaedi (koo-gad-ee) "mosquito"

Xax (hak; sometimes kak) "goose; likely an onomatopoeia of a goose's call"

Spider Woman Story

I have heard similar accounts of this narrative in the mythologies of other Alaska Native Peoples. Indeed, there are numerous stories involving Spider Woman in the mythologies of many American Indian tribes as well. This particular version was told to me at Culture Camp by Cecilia Larson, and later by her daughter, my cousin, Susan Larson.

There were these two Indian girls. One was smarter than the other. One day they were walking and they came to a waterfall. They started sliding down the hill and they forgot to go home. When they finally went home there was nobody there. There was nobody at their house. The girls looked all around camp, but there was no sight of their family.

Pretty soon, the girls asked some seagulls—*nalbaey*—if they knew where their mom and dad had gone. The birds said that they didn't know.

Then that Camprobber—*stakalbaey*—came around and they asked if he knew where their parents were.

"Can you tell us where our mom and dad have gone?" they asked. "We'll give you a necklace if you tell us," they said.

Stakalbaey took the necklace. That's why his neck is white. Then he told them what to do.

"Don't go on the wide road. Go on the narrow road." That's what he said to them.

After the bird flew away, the older sister started arguing with the younger sister saying, "We're supposed to go on the wide road. He said take the wide road." But the younger sister insisted that Camprobber had said to go on the narrow road. They argued like that for some time. Finally, though, the little girl gave up and went on the wide road because her older sister told her to.

67

A little ways down the wide road they came to a bad man. This old man— da'atnae—and his old wife were sitting in their cabin. He had a big pot cooking on the fire outside. Inside the pot he had dog eyes, bird eyes; all kinds of eyes boiling! The little girl became scared. Then the old man took an iron and put in the fire until it was really hot. Then he used it to kill the big girl. But when he was about to do the same thing to the younger sister, the smart little girl spoke to the old man.

"I want to go to the bathroom," she said.

The old man told her," No."

"I want to go to the bathroom. You can tie me around the waist with a rope and then let me go to the bathroom in the woods." That is what that smart young girl said to him.

The old woman gave her a comb for her hair. The girl put it into her pocket. Then she gave her other things too. The girl put them all into her pocket as well. Then the old woman told her to tie the rope to a stump. The young sister thanked her and then went out alone to go to the bathroom.

When she was far enough in the woods that the old man could no longer see her, the young girl untied herself and put the rope around a tree stump. Then she started running. She ran as fast as she could.

After enough time had passed, the old man yelled for the girl to return. When she did not answer he started to pull on the rope. He could feel her weight on it, but when he brought the rope all the way to camp he saw that it was only a stump. Oh, he was mad! He started running after that girl and yelling at her.

The frightened girl was running so fast that she dropped the comb and it turned into brush. She dropped many things while she was running, and whatever she dropped turned into things like hills and mountains and things. This slowed the man down.

Finally, she came upon a spider's house. It was Spider Woman's house. The young sister asked her for help.

"Can you tell me where my mom and dad have gone? I'm running from that old man who killed my sister," she said.

Spider Woman wrapped her up in a cocoon and hid her under her bed. When the old man came to the house he started knocking on the doors and windows. Spider Woman killed him somehow. When it was safe she started asking the girl questions.

"Do you want to see your family? You can see them," she said.

The smart young girl told her that she did want to see her parents again.

"See that big long rope? You need to fix it." That's what Spider Woman said to her.

The girl saw the rope made of spider's silk and agreed to fix it. Later, the woman told her to move a rock, but it was too big and she couldn't move it. That woman hit the rock with a stick and it went away. The girl looked at the hole where the rock had been and she could see her mom and dad all walking around. The girl began to cry. She wanted to go home.

Then Spider Woman took the thin, long rope that had been repaired and threw it down the hole after tying off one end.

"Do you want to go home now?" she asked.

The smart girl said that she did want to go home.

"Then I'm going to put you down on that string and you must close your eyes. If you open your eyes before the end you'll come back up here." That's what Spider Woman said.

Cecilia Larson

Before the girl reached the bottom of the rope she opened her eyes because she couldn't wait to see her family. But as soon as she did, she was right back at the top again and had to do it all over again. Finally, though, she climbed all the way down and her parents saw her. They were sad that her older sister was gone, but they were happy that their young, smart daughter was with them again.

nalbaey (nall-bay) "sea gull"

stakalbaey (stok-all-bay) "camprobber; gray jay"

da'atnae (daw-ot-na) "old man; not very old man, though"

Susan Larson and Ruth Johns

The Old Man and the Bear

This tale of respect may be more oral history than it is mythology. I have heard a similar account told by Tanacross Indians in the area near Tok, which is just outside of Ahtna Country. Although a narrative in both tribes, it may actually have been an Ahtna story first. Indeed, through intermarriage, many Indians in that area are of Ahtna descent.

Way up in northeastern Ahtna country, there is a story of a very Old Man—*nest'e'*—who lived in a small village where there is no village today. It may have only been a summer camp. It was midsummer and there were salmon everywhere. In all of the streams and rivers there were plenty of salmon—*łuk'ae.*

Some young boys wanted to go down by the river. This very Old Man asked if he could go with them. He was so old that he was bent over and used a stick when he walked. The boys didn't want the useless old man to go with them, but he did anyhow, and he was able to keep up with them.

They were walking down by the river when they saw a big grizzly—*tsaani.* Those boys started teasing the bear. They threw rocks and sticks at it and called it names.

"Tsaani, you are afraid of boys!" they laughed.

They had no respect for the bear. The very Old Man told them to stop, but the boys just kept on teasing that bear. They wouldn't listen to the man because he was so old.

Finally, the grizzly stopped and looked at them. Then it started walking towards them. When it came close the boys became afraid and ran away, leaving the old man to face the angry bear alone.

When it was very close, the bear charged the Old Man. The young boys thought surely the old man would be killed. But, when the bear

71

was almost upon him, the man stood as tall as he could and held his arms far apart with the walking stick in one hand. Then he yelled at the bear.

That bear didn't know what to think. He just stopped and sat down, his small dark eyes looking at the old man.

The very Old Man wasted no time. He hit the bear across the nose with his stick. That bear howled in pain and ran away. The old man had scared the bear away with only a walking stick!

The boys who had watched the whole thing from far away learned something that day. From then on they showed respect for elders and they never teased bears again.

nest'e' (nest-a) "very old man; not just an older man"

łuk'ae (thlook-a) "salmon [in general]"

tsaani (chaw-nee) "grizzly bear"

Three Generations of Ahtna

Owl Story

Just as parents told children about Bush Indians to keep them close to home and out of trouble, so too would they tell stories of Owl to keep small children from crying, especially at night. This narrative was by Markle Pete of Tazlina Village.

When I was a little boy, my parents told me stories about Owl—Besiini. They told us that we should never cry at night, especially if we were at camp. They said that Besiini hears crying children because he has such good hearing. Owl didn't like to hear crying children. That's what they told us Indian kids way back when I was growing up.

They said that if a crying child was in the woods, Owl would swoop down and cut off their feet. He would cut them off just below the ankles. He did this only to the children who were crying. Some of the stories were really scary. We were afraid to hear them sometimes.

One story said that a very young child, a baby really, was inside a house at night and crying. It cried and cried. That night Besiini flew in through an open window and took the baby away

Markle Pete of Tazlina

and ate it! Owl either cuts off children's feet, or kills them for crying too much!

I remember one night when I was a young boy. I had heard the

73

stories that day. I had thought about the stories all day long. I couldn't stop thinking about Besiini chasing after children to cut off their feet.

That night, when I was already in bed, I heard Owl outside my window.

"Whoo. Whoo." He must have been pretty close by.

I was so scared I jumped into bed with my mom and dad. My dad yelled at me, "What are you doing in our bed?"

I just crawled further under the blankets and said to my dad, "Hold on to my feet dad! Hold on to my feet!"

My parents just laughed and laughed.

Tazlina (Taz-lee-naw) "village and river name; swift water"

Besiini (bess-ee-nee) "Owl"

The Man With Too Many Wives

In my book, The Raven and the Totem, *I retold a similar story from Yupik (Central Eskimo) in which the wife turns into a bear to seek revenge by killing the unfaithful husband. In another Ahtna variation, the young woman is actually a mouse, dluuni.*

Long, long time ago, there was a man who had two wives. He would go hunting for days looking for food. He would be gone for many days at a time.

One day, while he was out hunting far from home, the man came upon a small house. It was the house of a beautiful, young single woman. He did not tell her that he had two wives. Because the woman thought that he was single too, she agreed to live with him in her house.

The man, who now had three wives in two different houses, would hunt for both households. He would bring only the best meat—*c'esten'*—to his new wife, and he brought only poor meat to his other two wives. It went on like that for a while—him living in one house for a few days and then in the other for a few days. Each time he would leave, the wives thought that he was only going hunting.

After a time, though, the two wives became suspicious.

"Why does our husband only bring us such poor meat?" they wondered.

One day the man returned with really poor moose meat. The women asked about the rest of the moose, but the husband said that it was all he got from the moose.

Next time that man left, one of the wives followed him. She followed him for most of a day until they came upon a house. As he approached, a beautiful, younger woman came out of the house and greeted the man. They both went inside and he did not come out for a long time.

As soon as he was gone, the first wife went up to the house. She introduced herself but did not mention that she was married to the same man.

"Where do you come from?" asked the young woman.

"I live far away. That is why you haven't seen me before," replied the older woman.

The younger, new wife was making oil from meat. She was boiling fat in a pot while they spoke.

The young wife started talking about how wonderful her new husband was—how he always brought her the best meat. The older woman became angry. Soon, she shoved the younger woman's head into the boiling pot of oil and killed her. Then she propped up her head with a stick so that it looked as if she was still stirring the boiling pot. Then she hid and waited.

When the husband came home he saw his new wife. It looked like she was stirring the cooking pot. He went over to hold her, but as he did she fell over. She was dead. The man cried and cried.

"My wife! My wife!" he kept saying.

The first wife who was hiding ran back to their house and told the other wife what had happened. When the man came home they did not let him know that they knew what had happened. But from then on he brought home only the best meat and the two women were happy.

dlunni (dloo-nee) "mouse"

c'esten' (ket-chen) "meat"

The House of Wind

This particular story teaches how to behave properly in society. I have heard several different versions (as with most stories), but this one is adapted from Atna' Yanida'a *as told by John Billum of Chitina.*

Once, long ago, Fox's daughter was married to Raven. They lived with her parents because they did not have a house of their own yet.

One day, while hunting far from home, Fox came upon a small house in the woods. He had never seen it before. There was no one around so he went inside. Everything was very neat and clean. There was lots of food, too.

"This is a very nice house," thought Fox.

He looked around but he touched nothing, and then he sat down to rest.

Soon a voice said, "What a good man he is. So honest. Surely he must be hungry. Let's give him something to eat."

That is what the voice said even though Fox didn't see anyone around that house. You see, it was the house of the Wind. Soon, food came flying to Fox. He ate things such as fish, meat, and berries—*gigi*. Everything tasted very good.

When it was time to leave, the voice spoke again.

"Let's give him something to take home."

Again, like before, things came flying to Fox. This time it was moose hides, necklaces, and moccasins—*kentsiis*. More meat also came to him. He put these things into his pack until it was very full. Before he left he thanked the voice and told them how much he liked their house—*hnax*. The pack was so heavy that Fox could barely carry it. When he returned home, Raven, his new son-in-law, saw the filled pack. He asked Fox where he got these things and Fox told him the story.

77

"Why didn't you just take everything since there was no one in the house?" asked Raven.

Fox replied, "It is not the right thing to do. You must sit still and touch nothing in someone else's home." That is what he said.

"If I had been there," said the Raven, "I would have taken everything."

The next day Raven said he was going to find the house. Fox told him to sit still and quiet and to touch nothing inside.

When Raven found the house, he went inside and asked aloud if there was anyone home. When no one answered he walked all over the house and ate all the food that was there and filled his pack with everything that he could.

Soon, he heard a voice.

"What a bad person you are. You just take whatever is not yours."

Raven went to where the sound came from and threw things at it. Then he quickly left the strange house. But before he was home, the wind picked up and a stick flew at him and hit his head, knocking him down hard. Then the pack was lifted by the wind and carried back to Wind's House.

Raven told Fox what had happened. Fox was not surprised. "You see," he said. "I told you not to touch anything and to sit still. It is wrong to take things like that."

gigi (gig-gee) "berry" [G pronounced as a cross between G and K]

kentsiis (ken-chees) "moccasins"

hnax (nock) "house"

How Raven Made Salmon Swim

This brief story illustrates how Raven made things the way they are. I have heard this story told by my grandmother, Mary Joe Smelcer, by Fred Ewan at Culture Camp in 1996, and by Katie John who told it to a group of Indian children while cutting salmon at her fish camp at Batzulnetas ("Roasted Salmon Place") in 1999. She cut the salmon head in half from its nose back to show us the rocks Raven put there.

Way long ago, before there were people, Raven had already created everything, including salmon. He had made the rivers and mountains, and the animals and birds. He created salmon to join the streams and rivers with the sea.

But even though Raven made salmon, they couldn't swim well because they weren't heavy enough. You see, they had a pocket of air inside their head. Because of this they would always float to the surface where they were too easy prey for Grizzly Bear—Tsaani—and Eagle—Sgulak.

One day when Raven was flying around, he noticed how much trouble salmon were having swimming and he decided to help them. He flew down to the chief of the Salmon People and spoke to him.

"Why is it that you seem to have so much trouble swimming?" he asked the fish.

The Chief of the Salmon People replied, "Our heads have air inside which makes us float. It is very hard to swim under water when our head keeps floating to the surface."

Raven thought about how to fix them. Then he lifted the chief of the Salmon People from the water and carefully placed a small stone inside

his head. When Raven replaced the fish into the Copper River, it sank
near the bottom and didn't float back to the surface.

"Tsin'aen," said the salmon to Raven, thanking him for what he had done.

From that time on, all salmon swim near the bottom of the rivers where they are not easy meals for other animals. When we cut them up for drying and smoking, we can still see the tiny rocks in their head which Raven put there long ago.

tsaani (chaw-nee) "grizzly bear"

sgulak (sgoo-lack) "eagle" [Alutiiq loanword]

tsin'aen (chin-nen) "thank you"

Fred Ewan

Katie John

When Raven Made Denali

Most long-time Alaskans still call the highest mountain in Alaska Mt. McKinley. But contemporary maps and the rest of the world call it Denali. At 20,320 feet tall, Denali can be seen from the hills around Fairbanks to the north and from the hills around Anchorage to the south. It is no wonder that something that so dominates the landscape has a story of its origin. Further, the word Denali may very well come from the Ahtna and neighboring Dena'ina language. The Ahtna word for mountain—dghelaay—sounds similar to the English pronunciation of Denali. The Ahtna village of Cantwell is close to the entrance of Denali National Park.

A very long time ago, when Raven was still creating the world, he got into an argument with Grizzly Bear. No one remembers what the argument was about, but it quickly turned into a fight. It was probably about food. Raven used his powers to make himself bigger than Grizzly Bear. But Grizzly Bear must have also had magical powers back then, because he made himself bigger as well. As the two wrestled, rolling in the dirt and shoving and tossing each other about, they made themselves bigger and bigger until they were almost as high as the clouds in the sky. They were giants. They were so big that the piles of dirt and rocks they kicked up during their struggle formed mountains, what today we call the Alaska Range. Denali was the highest mountain of all.

Denali

When They Killed the Monkey People

The story of the Cet'aeni—"The Long-Tailed Ones" or the "Monkey People" —is unique to Upper Ahtna oral history and does not appear in the stories of neighboring Indian tribes. This version, which differs from some accounts, was retold by Markle Pete and my grandmother, Mary Joe Smelcer. Another retelling can be found in Tatl'ahwt'aenn Nenn' (Ed. James Kari), as told by Fred John of Mentasta. I believe the name "Monkey People" is erroneous, applied only in recent years. We have no word for monkey in our language, nor any concept of monkeys, as they are not indigenous to the Americas. Based on the narratives and on observations, I believe the stories are actually about cougars, whose range historically extended into parts of Alaska. Indians of Iowa called cougars, "Long-Tails."

This story comes from upriver, mostly in the Mentasta area, but most Ahtna people have heard this story at one time or another.

A long time ago, but not back in yanida'a, maybe in the past couple hundred years, there were these long-tailed creatures living up around Batzulneta or around Slana. Somewhere up there. We called them Cet'aeni, or the "Monkey People."

These tailed-ones were kind of human-like. They walked on their hind legs, but they were hairy all over. They did not wear any clothes, and they had long tails.

It began that people started to disappear from this country. All kinds of people would disappear—children, old people, even young men and women, too. The Monkey People were killing them. It got so bad that Indians were afraid to go out alone. They were killing so many Ahtna that they might kill them all if they weren't stopped.

So, this one young man, who was brave and smart, he decided to find the Cet'aeni. He was very smart. One day after a man came running back to camp saying that he had seen a Tailed One near a treefall, the young man went there by himself.

He did not want the Cet'aeni to know that he was around, so he covered his footprints with grass. That way they could not see his tracks.

After a while, he came upon several Monkey People. There was a tree nearby so he climbed it. He climbed way up to the top so that the wind would carry his scent away. This way the Cet'aeni would not know that he was watching them.

Safe in his tree—ts'abaeli—the young man watched as the Monkey People played some game with what looked like a ball. But when he looked closer, he saw that it was really a human skull! They were throwing a human skull around like a ball! It was the skull of a young Indian man who had disappeared not long ago.

Just then it began to rain. The Tailed Ones didn't like the rain and so they started down the trail. The smart young man followed them, but he stayed far enough behind so that they did not know he was there.

After a while they came to a cliff by the river. Near the top of the cliff were eight caves, just big enough for a man to fit through. The Cet'aeni went up the side of the cliff and into the caves. That is where they lived.

The young man ran back to the village and told his people that he knew where they lived. The people gathered their spears and bows and arrows and left for the cliff with the cave in it. The women gathered dry branches and green branches along the way.

When they finally came to the caves, they saw many bones scattered all around the entrances. They were human bones! The women placed the dry branches in the entrances and lit a fire. As the fire grew hot, they threw green branches onto the fire. This made it begin to smoke. The dark smoke, made from the green boughs, filled the caves quickly.

Soon, the Monkey People began to come out of their houses. The smoke made it so that they could not see or breathe well. When they came out of the caves the Indian men killed them with spears and arrows and clubs. They killed all of them and only one Indian was killed in the battle. After that day, no more Ahtna people were killed by Cet'aeni. If they hadn't killed them, they surely would have killed all the Ahtna and then there would be no Indians in Copper River country—Atna'

Nen'—today.

People who have been in that area say that you can still see the cave up on the cliff just above the river. They say you can see smoke and charcoal remains there, too.

yanida'a (yan-i-da-a) "story time, mythics times"

Cet'aeni (Ket-tan-ee) "Monkey People, or Tailed Ones"

ts'abaeli (cha-bal-ee) "tree"

Atna' Nen' (aht-naw nen) "Copper River country"

The Boy Who Offended Salmon

In most cultures, the animals which provide food and clothing, although hunted or trapped, must be treated with respect. There are numerous Alaska Native myths which tell of these taboos, or in Ahtna, 'engii. Indeed, traditionally, adolescent children and menstruates were not allowed to handle salmon, and fresh caught fish could not be eaten until one day after its capture (big game meat, it was said, could not be eaten until three days after it had been killed). A version of this narrative was first recorded by Fredrica de Laguna.

Once there was a young Indian boy who lived in a small village along the river. As with most Ahtna communities, most of the villagers were relatives and members of his clan.

During the summer, all the adults were busy catching salmon— *łuk'ae*—which they would smoke and dry or boil to make fish oil. This is how things were back then. Everyone worked to put away food for winter. Without salmon, people would surely starve in winter. They used almost all of the fish. They even made fishhead soup from it.

It is important to show respect for the salmon. If we offend them by wasting their flesh, then they might not come again next year. If we did not return their bones to the river so that their spirits could rejoin their kin, then they might not return as well. Salmon are so important that June is called Łuk'ae Na'aaye'.

Although young children could not handle freshly-caught fish, and they could not cut it up for hanging on drying racks, they were often-times asked to throw the fish bones back into the river after the meat had been eaten. This one boy was lazy and disrespectful. One day he was asked to throw a bunch of fish bones back into the river. But because it was further than he cared to walk, that boy just went in the woods behind his house and threw the bones onto the dirt. He kicked some more dirt upon them to cover up what he had done. Later that night, when he was given a piece of dried salmon, he complained that he was tired of fish and he threw it into the fire when no one was looking.

Soon the salmon run became very small. Fewer and fewer fish were caught in nets each day. The people began to worry that there would not be enough salmon put away for winter.

Each day, when asked to return the fish bones to the river, that boy would throw them on the ground instead. Sometimes he would just cover them up with a few branches or twigs. Each time he did this, fewer salmon were caught the next day.

One day, the boy was walking a little ways from fish camp when he heard something talking from the river. It was a voice calling to him. He walked over to where it came from, but he saw nothing. Then the voice came from upriver a little ways. It came from below a steep bank at the river's edge. The boy lay upon his belly and hung over the edge to see who it was speaking to him from the water. Just then the bank gave way, and the boy fell into the dark, swift water.

It was the Salmon Chief—Łuk'ae Kaskae—who had tricked him. Now that boy was taken by the Salmon People for what he had done to their relatives.

'engii (en-gee) "taboo, that which is forbidden"

Łuk'ae Na'aaye' (Thlook-a Naw-eye) "Salmon Month"

Łuk'ae Kaskae (Thloo-ka Kass-ka) [pronounce a as in "cat"] "Salmon Chief"

When Raven Killed Porcupine

This story was originally told by Jake Tansy of Cantwell, the northwestern-most Ahtna village located just outside of Denali National Park. Jake was born at Valdez Creek in 1906. A similar version of this story appeared in Indian Stories *(1982), a small limited printing bilingual collection of Cantwell Indian stories.*

A long time ago, just like today, Indians hunted porcupine (*nuuni*). But long ago, some people way up near Tyone Lake would go hunting for porcupines and never return. They just disappeared. The villagers became scared, so they planned a war against the porcupine who must be killing all of the hunters.

Raven heard their plans and decided to go find that porcupine himself. He flew down the Tyone River into upper Susitna country until he came to where the *nuuni* lived. Way up in a tree sat the very big porcupine eating bark. It was truly the biggest porcupine he had ever seen.

Raven hid behind some bushes and waited until he came down from the tree. When Porcupine finally came down, Raven walked over to him quietly. Nuuni heard something behind him and flared out his quills. He had many long, sharp quills—*c'ok*— on his back.

Raven stopped and spoke to him.

"I came to tell you something important," he said.

"What news did you bring me?" asked Porcupine.

Raven told him that the villagers planned a war against him. He told him that they were even now gathering upriver preparing for war with many bows and arrows.

Porcupine was worried.

"What should I do?" he asked.

That tricky Raven had an idea.

"Are you skillful enough to catch their arrows as they shoot them at you?"

"I don't know," said Nuuni.

Raven told the porcupine that he would train him. He started by shooting an arrow at him very slowly. It was so slow that Porcupine easily caught it. Then Raven shot the next arrow slightly faster. Each time Nuuni caught the arrow—*cenk'a'*—in the air and was unharmed. They trained like that all day until Raven was shooting arrows very fast and Porcupine was able to catch them without being hurt.

Then Raven shot at a stump just to the side of the big porcupine and struck it in the middle. The arrow was shot fast and it stuck deep into the stump.

Nuuni went over to take out the arrow. While he was trying to pull it from the stump, Raven aimed and shot Porcupine below the armpit near where his heart was, killing him. He died because he was shot in his *ciz'aani*, his heart.

Raven flew down to where the villagers gathered and told them what he had done. From then on, no villagers were killed when they went porcupine hunting.

nuuni (new-nee) "porcupine"

c'ok (kee*awk) "quills" [*pronounced as one syllable]

cenk'a' (kenk-a) "arrow" [a pronounced as in 'cat']

ciz'aani (kiz-aw-nee) "heart"

The Woman Taken By A Bear

This story was also originally told by Jake Tansy of Cantwell in Indian Stories *(1982). His daughter, Lousie Tansy Mayo, translated the narratives from western Ahtna dialect into English. In many Athabaskan storytelling traditions, there are stories of bears abducting and even marrying women.*

There was a potlatch a long time ago. It was a big potlatch and everyone was invited. People were sent to tell neighboring villages about it. Even Bear—*tsaani*— was told about it.

In the village where the potlatch was held, there lived a beautiful young woman. Bear saw her go inside the sweathouse alone. While she was still inside, Tsaani reached in and pulled her out by her long, black hair. Then he ran away from the village with her. He took her up to a mountain ridge before he stopped.

"This is my home," he said. "Stay close to the fire and don't run away." That is what he told her.

The woman didn't run away because she didn't even know where she was. Bear went off to get some cooking sticks. After he was out of sight, the girl looked around the camp. She saw a mouse—*dluuni*— nearby and it spoke to her.

"That bear is really a bad person," it said. "You must get away from him. I will help you."

Dluuni gave her a feather and a sewing needle which she put in her hair. Then he gave her some meat.

A little later, Tsaani came back with roasting sticks, *gges*. He saw the meat and cooked some to eat. He had planned to eat the woman,

93

but he ate the meat for now. When they had eaten, he said they would
go down to a nearby lake. They went down the mountain to the lake
which was frozen. It was barely frozen, though. You could see right
through it. The ice was still thin.

"You walk out on the lake first and then I will," said Bear.

As the beautiful woman walked out towards the middle of the lake—
ben—the ice began to sag and make cracking sounds. But because she
was wearing the feather that mouse had given her, she did not break
through. She had become light because of the feather—*t'aa*.

She walked back to the edge. Now it was Tsaani's turn. That big
bear walked slowly and carefully, but when he was in the middle of
the lake he fell through the ice. The water was deep and cold and Bear
could not get out. He was in trouble. He asked the girl to help him.

"If you help me, I will take you home," he said. That is what he
promised. He made a promise.

But after the girl helped him, Bear forgot all about what he had said
and he did not take her home to her people.

The next day he took her down to the lake again. This time, when
she was half way across, Bear stomped his foot and said, "Lake, be a
lake again."

Suddenly the ice became even thinner and one of the girl's feet fell
through. She carefully lifted her foot out of the water and walked back
to shore because of her feather.

When it was Bear's turn, the young woman waited until he was in
the middle and then she stomped her foot and said, "Be a lake again."

Suddenly the ice became very thin and Bear fell through. Again he
promised to take the girl home if she pulled him out.

"No, you promised me that yesterday and you didn't take me home,"
replied the woman who had been taken by the bear.

"This time I'm telling the truth," he said. "I promise to take you
home."

The woman helped him out of the water. After Bear dried off, he
lowered his back so that she could sit on him, and they started off with
her on his back. But it wasn't really the trail to her village. Instead,
it was the path to Bear's nephews' house. When he was close to their
house, Tsaani told her to walk the rest of the way by herself. He knew
that his nephews would eat her when she came upon them up the trail.

A little later, she came upon Bear's hungry nephews. They chased
her, but before they caught her she turned into a feather! She became

a feather. The bears jumped up to get her, but they could not catch her. Then, while she was a feather in the air, that woman turned into a long sewing needle and she pierced the bears in the heart, killing them. Then she turned back into a person again.

When she had walked down the trail a ways, she came upon Tsaani. He was very surprised that she was still alive. He thought that she must have somehow killed his nephews. This scared Bear who thought maybe she could kill him, too.

Finally, Bear agreed to take her home. He put her on his back and carried her across the country and over the mountain until she was home again.

Tsaani (chaw-nee) "grizzly bear"

dluuni (dloo-nee) "mouse"

gges (gess) "roasting stick"

ben (ben) "lake"

t'aa (k-taw) "feather" [pronounced as two syllables]

Giant Killer

Stories of little people and of giants are found in the folklore and mythologies of many world cultures. Consider the American folktale of Paul Bunyan and Blue Babe. These stories exist in the narratives of such distant and diverse culture as Irish and Eskimo; in the European accounts of gnomes, trolls, and borrowers; and in the oral traditions of Ahtna. This story was narrated by John Billum in Chitina and published in Atna' Yanida'a.

In the far time, when things were not as they are today, there lived in Indian country a giant man and a giant woman. While the man never harmed the little Ahtna People, the woman giant was always killing them, like ants—*nadosi*—beneath her feet.

One day a young Indian man was hunting. He found a porcupine den and he crawled inside to catch the nuuni that lived there. While he was inside a shadow fell across the entrance and blocked the sunlight. The young man wondered what it could be that blocked the sun. He looked out the hole and saw this giant man.

"Come out and talk to me," said the giant.

The Indian was scared. He had never before seen a giant, though he had heard stories about them and how Indians were killed by them.

"I am Nigi Giidzi," said the giant. "Come out from the den. I need your help. I will not harm you."

The young man crawled out from the den and stood in front of the giant, barely coming up to his knees.

"What can I do to help you?" asked the Indian.

The giant named Nigi Giidzi told him about the woman giant. He told him how she always killed the little Indians. He told him that he wanted to kill her, but that she was too strong and cunning to defeat on his own.

"While I am fighting with her, you will come out from a hiding place and cut the tendons of her heel. Then she will not be able to stand up and I will be able to get rid of her."

That is what the giant said to the little man.

The Indian agreed, and so Nigi Giidzi placed him upon his shoulder and they walked for a long time until they found the giant woman eating several mountain sheep.

The two giants fought, and the little man helped the giant get rid of the woman giant and all of the little people were saved.

nadosi (na-doe-see) "ant" [specifically: carpenter ant]

nuuni (new-nee) "porcupine"

The First Mosquitoes

This is another popular giant story, which appears in the folklore of other Alaska Native cultures. Mosquitoes are the bane of existence during the Alaskan warm, snow-free months. It has been calculated that the biomass of all mosquitoes is greater than the combined mass of all other living things in Alaska, including every animal, bird, and fish. Birds from around the world migrate to Alaska every summer to feast on the swarms. There are accounts of Klondike gold miners killing themselves to escape the relentless torment. As ubiquitous as mosquitoes are—from the rainforests of southeast Alaska to the Arctic plains—it is no wonder that there are stories about their origins. This version was told to me by Fred Stickwan.

Long ago, there was a giant who killed and ate Indians. He was especially fond of drinking their blood. He killed so many Indians that the people became concerned that they might be wiped out. None of the young men who went off to fight the giant ever returned. The bloodthirsty giant killed them all and ate them, roasting their hearts on a fire.

But one especially smart and brave young man said, "I will kill the giant and save our village."

The young man was the youngest of three brothers. His two older brothers had died trying to kill the giant, and he wanted to avenge their deaths. The young man followed the giant's tracks for several days until he found the cave where he lived. Human bones were piled outside the cave. The young man lay down close to the entrance, pretending to be dead, and waited. Shortly, the giant came outside, following a scent he smelled. He saw the young man lying there on the trail. He touched him.

"Still warm," he said. "These humans are making it so easy for me. Now they die right on my trail from fear of me."

The giant picked up the young man who was pretending to be dead and threw him over his hairy shoulder and carried him into the cave. He dropped him right beside the smoldering campfire. The young man fell flat on his stomach with one arm beneath his chest. Then the giant went back outside to gather firewood so he could cook the man and roast his heart on a stick. Quickly, for there was little time to waste, the young man took his knife and clutched it in his hand that was beneath his chest so that the giant could not see the knife. The giant returned and tossed the firewood onto the fire and blew on it until it was aflame. Then he grabbed the Indian and picked him up. He was just about to bite off the young man's head so he could drink his blood, when the young man slashed the giant's throat with his knife.

With his dying breath the giant cursed the Indian.

"Though you have killed me, I'm going to keep drinking your blood forever."

After the giant was dead, the young man cut up the giant's body and burned it. When the last piece was burned down to ashes, he scooped up all the ashes and took them outside and flung them into the air to scatter them on the winds. Instantly, every speck of ash turned into a mosquito. It was a giant cloud of

Fred Stickwan

kuggaedi (mosquitoes), the very first ones. Many of them landed on the young man and bit him, sucking his blood. The young man ran home, chased by the cloud of mosquitoes. From that day, mosquitoes have tormented humans.

kuggaedi (koo-gad-dee) "mosquito"

The Hole in the Sky

Over the decades, my grandmother, Mary Joe Smelcer, and my great aunt, Morrie Secondchief, told me many stories. Both were born not long after first contact with Europeans and were raised before Christianity got a foothold in their region. While most coastal Alaska Native communities had already converted to Russian Orthodox—frequently at gunpoint after years of slaughter and enslavement by the Russians—it took much longer for western religions to make their way into the interior. As such, my grandmother and her sister grew up hearing only the old stories. But eventually Christianity pushed its way into every corner of Alaska, including into Ahtna Country. It must have been a difficult time, as the old Ways of Knowing gave way to a new way. It didn't help that missionaries frequently degraded the traditional stories as being superstitious and devil-worship. Consequently, my grandmother, even in her seventies, sometimes unintentionally merged both the old and the new. She might be talking about a time Raven did this or that to Wolf and Fox, and a moment later refer to them as Jesus and the disciples. I'd ask her if she knew what she had done, and she'd insist that she hadn't. I'd replay the videotape to show her. In any case, the following story told to me by my grandmother in 1992 is clearly a blending of traditional myth-telling and Christianity.

A long time ago, two hunters were out hunting in the middle of winter. They were snowshoeing along a frozen river beneath the starry sky when they saw something strange up ahead. When they were closer, they saw that it was a hole torn in the sky. Some old folks used to say that night is just a giant black blanket that Raven throws over the world to make it nighttime. The stars we see are where light comes through little pin-holes in the blanket.

The two hunters were afraid but curious.

They took off their snowshoes and approached the hole with their bows drawn back. The hole must have been about eight feet off the ground. So one man cupped his hands together like this and the other man put his foot there and then that first man he heaved the other man up so he could look inside that hole.

Well, the man looked into that hole and he saw it was Heaven. He leaned over and told his friend what he saw and described how beautiful it was. That man on the ground said, "It's my turn. Let me look." But that man just kept looking and then finally he crawled into that hole and disappeared. He didn't even help his friend up or say good-bye. He just forgot about this world and wanted to be in Heaven. I guess lots of people just want to be in Heaven.

Bibliography

Preface to Bibliographic Index

Although texts about Alaska Native Oral Narratives have been published throughout the world, several publishers appearing in this Bibliographic Index have produced the greatest volume of works in publication. To simplify the task of documenting those sources within this bibliography, I have abbreviated their titles as follows:

A.C.C. Anchorage Community College (now part of the University of Alaska Anchorage)

A.L.L. Adult Literacy Laboratory, Anchorage, Alaska

A.N.L.C. Alaska Native Language Center, University of Alaska Fairbanks

I.A.S.D. Iditarod Area School District, McGrath, Alaska

L.K.S.D. Lower Kuskokwim School District, Bethel, Alaska

N.B.M.D.C. National Bilingual Materials Development Center, Rural Education Extension, Anchorage, Alaska

Bibliographic Index of Alaska Native Oral Narratives and Ethnography

Aleut

Alaska Quarterly Review, vol. 4, no. 3 & 4. Ed. Tom Sexton, Ron Spats, James J. Liszka. Anchorage: University of Alaska Anchorage, 1986.

Bernet, Jack W., ed. *An Anthology of Aleut, Eskimo, and Indian Literature of Alaska*. Fairbanks: University of Alaska Fairbanks, English Department, 1974.

Chugach Legends: Stories and Photographs of the Chugach Region. Anchorage: Chugach Corporation, 1984.

Dumond, Donald. *The Eskimos and Aleuts*. London: Thames and Hudson, 1977.

Golder, F. A. "Aleutian Stories" in *The Journal of American Folklore*, vol. 18, No. 70 (July-September 1905), pp. 215-222.

Jochelson, Waldemar. *Aleut Tales and Narratives*. Ed. Knut Bergsland. Fairbanks: A.N.L.C., 1990.

———. *Aleut Traditions*. Retrans. Knut Bergsland. Fairbanks: A.N.L.C., 1977.

Lynch, Kathleen. *Stories of the Aleutians*. Anchorage: A.L.L. / A.C.C., 1978.

Sawden, Feona. *Qangirllat Picit (Old Beliefs)*. Anchorage: N.B.M.D.C., 1979.

Selections from Aleut folklore. Alaska Bilingual Education Center, 1976.

Smelcer, John. "The First Seals" in *Missouri Folklore Society*, May 2014. *http://missourifolkloresociety.truman.edu/smelcer%2520two%252-0narratives.htm*

Stories of the Aleutians and Kodiak. Anchorage: A.L.L., 1978.

Torrey, Barbara B. *Slaves of the Harvest*. St. Paul Island: Tanadgusix Corporation, 1978.

Unangum ungiikangin kayux tunusangin (Aleut tales and narratives). Fairbanks: A.N.L.C., 1990.

Yachmeneff, Alexey M. *Unagam ungiikangin (Aleut Traditions)*. Fairbanks: A.N.L.C., 1976.

Athabaskan

Alaska Quarterly Review. Vol. 4, No. 3 & 4. Ed. Tom F. Sexton, Ronald Spatz, James J. Liszka. Anchorage: University of Alaska Anchorage, 1986.

Allen, Henry T. *Report of an Expedition to the Copper, Tanana, and Koyukon Rivers, in the Territory of Alaska, in the Year 1885.* Washington: GPO, 1887

Attla, Catherine. *As My Grandfather Told It: Traditional Stories from the Koyukuk.* Alaska: Yukon-Koyukuk School District and the Alaska Native Language Center (UAF), 1983.

——. *Stories We Lived By: Traditional Koyukon Athabaskan Stories.* Fairbanks: Alaska Native Language Center (UAF) and the Yukon-Koyukuk School District. 1989.

Bernet, John W., ed. *An Anthology of Aleut, Eskimo, and Indian Literature of Alaska.* Fairbanks: University of Alaska Fairbanks, 1974.

Bernet, Jack and James Ruppert (eds.) *Our Voices: Stories from Native Alaska and the Yukon.* Lincoln: Nebraska UP, 2001.

Boas, Franz, ed. *Mythology and Folk-Tales of N. American Indians.* American Ethnological Society. Leiden: E. J. Brill, 1914.

Brean, Alice. *Athabascan Stories.* Anchorage: Alaska Methodist UP, 1975.

Chapman, John W. *Athabaskan Stories from Anvik.* Ed. And Trans. James Kari. Fairbank: A.N.L.C., 1981.

——. "Athabascan Traditions from the Lower Yukon." *Journal of American Folklore* 15, no. 62 (1903): 180-85.

——. *Tena Texts and Tales from Anvik, Alaska.* American Ethnological Society No. 6 Leiden: E. J. Brill. 1914.

Cruickshand, Julie. *Athabaskan Women: Lives and Legends.* Ottawa: Canadian National Museum of Man, Mercury Series, Ethnology Service Paper No. 57, 1979.

De Laguna, Frederica, and Marie-Francoise Guedon. "Ahtna Field Notes." Manuscripts in author's possession. Microfilm copy at American Philosophical Society, Philadelphia, 1968.

Deacon, Belle. *Their Stories of Long Ago.* Ed. James Kari. Fairbanks: A.N.L.C. and the Iditarod Area School District, 1987.

DOTSON' SA TAALEEBAAY LAATLGHAAN (How Raven Killed The Whale). Trans. Eliza Jones. Fairbanks: A.N.L.C. (Date unknown)

Dundes, Alan. *Folklore Theses and Dissertations in the United States*. Austin: Texas UP, 1976.

Ellanna, Linda J. and Andrew Balluta. *Nuvendatin Quht'ana: The People of Nondalton*. Washington: Smithsonian, 1992.

Erdoes, Richard and Alfonso Ortiz (eds). *American Indian Myths and Legends*. New York: Pantheon Books, 1984.

Fast, Phyllis A. *Naatsilanei and Ko'ehdan: A Semiotic Analysis of Two Alaska Native Myths*. MFA thesis. Anchorage: University of Alaska Anchorage, 1990.

Fredson, John and Edward Sapir. *Kutchin texts with translations*. Ethnology Division Archives. National Museum Of Man, Ottawa, Canada, 1923.

Greene, Diana S. *Raven Tales & Medicine Men: Folktales from Eagle Village*. 1988. (No other data available)

Guedon, Marie-Francoise. *People of Tetlin, Why Are You Singing?* Canadian National Museum of Ma, Mercury Series, Ethnology Service Paper No. 9, Ottawa, 1974.

Henry, Chief and Eliza Jones. *K'ooitsaah Ts'in' (Koyukon Riddles)*. Fairbanks: A.N.L.C., 1977.

Herbert, Belle. *Shandaa: In My Lifetime*. Ed. Bill Pfisterer. Fairbanks: A.N.L.C., 1982.

Jette, Jules. "On Ten'a Folk-Lore." *Journal of the Royal Anthropological Institute of Great Britain and Ireland*. N.s., 38 (1908):298-367; 39 (1909):406-505.

Kalifornsky, Peter. *K'TL'EGH'I SUKDUA (Remaining Stories)*. Fairbanks: A.N.L.C., 1984.

Kari, James. ed. *A Dena'ina Legacy: The Collected Writings of Peter Kalifornsky*. Fairbanks: A.N.L.C., 1991.

——. *Tatl'ahwt' aenn Nenn': The Headwaters People's Country*. Fairbanks: A.N.L.C., 1986.

——. *Ts'eba Tthadala'. The First Christmas Tree Story*. Fairbanks: A.N.L.C., 1991.

Keim, Charles J., Ed. "Kutchin Legends From Old Crow." *Anthropological Papers of the University of Alaska* 1 1 (1964): 9.

Krauss, Michael E., Ed. *Native Peoples and Languages of Alaska (Map)*. Fairbanks: A.N.L.C., 1974. Reprinted 1982.

Krenov, Julia. "Legends from Alaska." *Journal de la Societe des Americanistes*. n.s., 40 (1951): 173-95.

Lohr, Amy L., ed. *Athabaskan Story-Teaching: Gaither D. Paul Stories.* Alaska Historical Commission Studies in History, No. 183, 1985.

Mackenzie, Clara C. *Zhoh Gwatsan: Wolf Smeller.* Anchorage: Alaska Pacific UP, 1985.

Mishler, Craig. ed. *Kutchin Tales.* Trans. Moses P. Gabriel. Anchorage: Adult Literacy Library, 1973.

———. *Born With the River: An Ethnography and Ethnohistory of Alaska's Big Delta-Goodpaster Indians.* Anchorage: Alaska Department of Natural Resources. 1984.

Nelson, Richard K. *Make Prayers to the Raven: A Koyukon View of the Northern Forest.* Chicago: Chicago Press, 1989.

Norman, Howard. *Northern Tales: Traditional Stories of Eskimo and Indian Peoples.* New York: Pantheon. 1990.

Osgood, Cornelius. *Contributions to the Ethnography of the Kutchin.* New Haven: Yale University Publication in Anthropology, No. 14 (1936), 1970.

———, *The Ethnography of the Tanaina.* New Haven: Yale University Publication in Anthropology, 1937.

Paul, Gaither. *Stories for my Grandchildren.* Ed. Ron Scollon. Fairbanks: A.N.L.C., 1980.

Peter, Katherine and Mary L. Pope. ed. *Dinjie Zhuu Gwandak: Gwich'in Stories.* Anchorage: Alaska State Operated Schools, 1974. Reprint.

Peters, Henry. *NAY' NADELIGHA I'GHAAN DGHSAT 'AEN'DEN (The War at Nay'nadeli).* Trans. and ed. James Kari. Fairbanks; A.N.L.C., 1977.

Q'udi Heyi Nilch'diluyi Sukdu'a (This Year's Collected Stories). Trans. and ed. James Kari. Anchorage: N.B.M.D.C., 1980.

Ridley, Ruth. *EAGLE HAN HUCH'INN HODOK (Stories in Eagle Han Huch'inn).* Fairbanks: A.N.L.C., 1983.

Schmitter, Ferdinand. *Upper Yukon Native Customs and Folk-Lore.* Washington: Smithsonian Collections, Vol. 56, No. 4, 1906. Reprinted 1985.

Sheppard, Janice R. "The Dog-Husband: Structural Identity and Emotional Specificity in Northern Athapaskan Oral Narrative." *Arctic Anthropology* 26. 1983.

Smelcer, John. *In the Shadows of Mountains: Stories from the Copper River Indians.* Glennallen, Ahtna Heritage Foundation, 1997.

——. *Alaska Native Oral Narrative Literature: A Guidebook and Bibliographic Index.* Anchorage: Ahtna Native Corporation, 1992.

——. "When Raven Killed Grizzly Bear" in *Missouri Folklore Society*, May 2014. *http://missourifolkloresociety.truman.edu/smelcer%2520two-%2520narratives.htm*

Tansy, Jake. *Hwtsaay Hwt'aene Yenida'a: Stories of the Small Timber People, The Ahtna People of the Upper Susitua River-Upper Gulkana River Country.* (Ed. James Kari & Millie Buck). 1982, reprinted by Ahtna Heritage Foundation in 1997.

Tildzidza Hwzoya' (Mouse Story). Told by Alta Jerue. Trans. Betty Petruska. McGrath: Iditarod Area School District, 1990.

Tenenbaum, Joan M. *Denan'ina Sukdu'a: Traditional Stories of the Tanaina Athabaskans.* Ed. Mary J. McGary. Fairbanks: A.N.L.C., 1984.

Vaudrin, Bill. *Ranaina Tales from Alaska.* Norman: Oklahoma UP, 1969.

Wassillie, Albert, Jr. *Nuvendaltun Ht'ana Sukdu'a (Nondalton People's Stories).* Ed. James Kari. Anchorage: N.B.M.D.C., 1980.

Eskimo

Ager, Lynn P. "Storytelling: an Alaskan Eskimo Girl's Game." *Journal of the Folklore Institute* 11. no. 3 (1974): 189-98.

Alaska Quarterly Review. vol. 4. no. 3 & 4. Ed. Tom F. Sexton. Ronald Spatz. James J. Liszka. Anchorage: University of Alaska Anchorage, 1986.

Balikci, Asen. *The Netsilik Eskimo.* Garden City: Natural History Press, 1970.

Bergsland, Knut. ed. *Nunamiut Stories.* Barrow: North Slope Borough Commission on Inupiat History, 1987.

Bernet, John W., ed. *An Anthology of Aleut, Eskimo, and Indian Literature of Alaska.* Fairbanks: University of Alaska Fairbanks, 1974.

Bernet, Jack and James Ruppert (eds.) *Our Voices: Stories from Native Alaska and the Yukon.* Lincoln: Nebraska UP, 2001.

Birket-Smith, Kaj. *The Chugach Eskimo.* Cøpenhagen: National Museets Publikationsfønd. 1953.

Boas, Franz. "The Central Eskimo." *6th Annual Report of the Bureau of American Ethnology for the Years 1884-1885.* Washington. 1888. Reprint. Lincoln: Nebraska UP, 1964.

———. *Mythology and Folktales of N. American Indians.* American Ethnological Society. Leiden: E. J. Brill, 1914.

Bogoras, Waldemar. *Materials for the Study of the Chukchee Language and Folklore.* St. Petersburg: Imperial Academy of Science, 1900.

———. *The Eskimo of Siberia.* Trans. Waldemar Borgoras. New York; AMS Press, 1987.

———. *The Longest Story Ever Told.* Anchorage: Alaska Pacific UP, 1981.

Carius, Helen S. *Sevukakmet.* Anchorage: Alaska Pacific UP, 1979.

Chugach Legends: Stories and Photographs of the Chugach Region. John F. C. Johnson, Compiler. Anchorage: Chugach Alaska Corporation, 1984.

Collins, Henry B. "Descriptions of the Polar Eskimo." *Handbook of North American Indians,* vol. 5. Washington: Smithsonian (1985): 8.

DeArmond, Dale. *Berry Woman's Children.* New York: Greenwillow Books, 1985.

———. *The Boy Who Found the Light.* Boston: Little, Brown & Company, 1990.

———. *The First Man: An Eskimo Folktale from Point Hope.* Sitka: Old Harbor Press, 1990.

Erdoes, Richard and Alfonso Ortiz (eds). *American Indian Myths and Legends.* New York: Pantheon Books, 1984.

Hansen, Susan K. *Yupik Eskimo Cultural History and Lore From The Lower Yukon River.* Fairbanks: 1985.

Jenness, Diamond. "Myths and Traditions from Northern Alaska, the Mackenzie Delta, and Coronation Gulf." *Report of Canadian Arctic Expedition,* 1913-1918.

Kawagley, Dolores. *Yupik Stories.* Anchorage: Alaska Methodist UP, 1975.

Keithahn, Edward L. *Alaskan Igloo Tales.* Seattle: Robert D. Seal, 1958.

Krauss, Michael E. *Native Peoples and Languages of Alaska (Map).* Fairbanks: Alaska Native Language Center, 1982.

Krenov, Julia. "Legends from Alaska." *Journal de la Societe des Americanistes.* n.s., 40 (1951): 173-95.

Lantis, Margaret. "The Mythology of Kodiak Island, Alaska." *Journal of American Folklore* 51, No. 200 (1938): 123-72.

Legends and Stories: Unipchaailiu Uqaaqtuallu. Trans. Ruth R. Sampson. Anchorage: N.B.M.D.C., 1976.

Legends and Stories: Unipchaallu Uqaaqtuailu 11. Trans. Ruth R. Sampson. Anchorage: N.B.M.D.C., 1978.

Long, Orma F. *Eskimo Legends*. Hicksville: Exposition Press, 1978.

Lowenstein, Tom. *Ancient Land: Sacred Whale*. New York: Farrar, Strauss & Giroux, 1993.

Lucier, Charles B. "Noatagmiut Eskimo Myths." *Anthropological Papers of the University of Alaska* 6, No. 2 91958): 89-117.

Lynch, Kathleen. *Northern Eskimo Stories*. Anchorage: Adult Literacy Laboratory, Anchorage Community College, 1978.

Maher, Ramona. *The Blind Boy and the Loon and Other Myths*. New York: John Day, 1969.

Mayokook, Robert. *Eskimo Stories*. Anchorage.

McCorckle, Ruth. *The Alaska Ten Footed Bear and Other Legends*. Seattle: Robert D. Seal, 1958.

Millman, Lawrence. *A Kayak Full Of Ghosts: Eskimo Tales*. Santa Barbara: Capra Press, 1987.

Murdoch, John. "A Few Legendary Fragments from Point Barrow Eskimos." *American Naturalists* 20. 1986.

Nanogake, Agnes. *More Tales from the Igloo*. Edmonton: Hurtig, 1986.

Nelson, Edward W. "The Eskimo about Bering Strait." *18th Annual Report of the Bureau of American Ethnology*. Washington: GPO, 1899.

Norman, Howard. *Northern Tales: Traditional Stories of Eskimo and Indian Peoples*. New York: Pantheon Books, 1990.

Oman, Lela Kiana. *Eskimo Legends*. Anchorage: Alaska Methodist UP, 1975.

Oquilluk, William A. *People of Kauwerak: Legends of the Northern Eskimo*. Anchorage: Alaska Methodist UP, 1973.

Rasmussen, Knud. *The Eagle's Gift: Alaska Eskimo Tales*. Trans. Isobel Hutchinson. New York: Doubleday & Doran. 1932.

——. *Eskimo Folk Tales*. Ed. and Trans. W. Worster. Cøpenhagen: Gyldendal, 1921.

Rink, Hinrich J. *Tales and Traditions Of The Eskimo*. Ed. Robert Brown. London: William Blackwood & Sons, 1875.

Rink, Signe. "The Girl and the Dogs: An Eskimo Folktale." *American Anthropologist*. 1898.

Silook, Roger S. *Seevookuk: Stories the Old People Told on St. Lawrence Island*. Anchorage: Alaska Publishing Company, 1976.

Smelcer, John E. *Alaska Native Oral Narrative Literature: A Guidebook and Bibliographic Index*. Anchorage: Ahtna Native Corporation, 1992.

Spencer, Robert F. *The Northern Alaskan Eskimo: A Study in Ecology and Society. Bureau of American Ethnology Bulletin.* No. 171. Washington, 1959. Reprinted in 1969.

Stefansson, Vilhjalmur. "Report of Stefansson-Anderson Arctic Expeditions." *Anthropological Papers of the American Museum of Natural History.* Vol. XIV. New York, 1919.

Sverdrup, Harald U. *Among The Tundra People.* Trans. Molly Sverdrup. Regents of University of California, 1978.

Tennant, Edward A. and Joseph N. Bitar, ed. *Yupik Lore: Oral Traditions of an Eskimo People.* Bethel: L.K.S.D., 1981.

Trask, Willard R. *The Unwritten Song.* New York: Macmillan, 1967.

Whittaker, C. E. *Arctic Eskimo: A Record of Fifty Years' Experience & Observation among the Eskimo.* London: Seeley, Service & Co., 1937. Reprinted 1976.

Wilder, Edna. *Once Upon an Eskimo Time.* Edmonds: Alaska Northwest Publishing Company, 1987.

Woodbury, Anthony C. *CEV'ARMIUT QANEMCIIT QULIRAIT-LLU: Eskimo Narratives and Tales from Chevak, Alaska.* Fairbanks: University of Alaska Press, 1984.

——. *Life in the Quasgiq, In Inua: Spirit World of the Bering Sea Eskimo.* Washington: Smithsonian, 1982.

Eyak

Alaska Quarterly Review, vol. 4, no. 3 & 4. Ed. Tom Sexton, Ron Spatz, and James J. Liszka. Anchorage: University of Alaska Anchorage, 1986.

Allen, Henry T. *Report of an Expedition to the Copper, Tanana, and Koyukon Rivers, in the Territory of Alaska, in the year 1885.* Washington: GPO, 1887.

De Laguna, Frederica and Kaj Birket-Smith. *The Eyak Indians of The Copper River Delta.* Cøpenhagen, 1938.

Norman, Howard. *Northern Tales.* New York: Pantheon, 1990.

Krauss, Michael. *In Honor of Eyak.* Fairbanks: Alaska Native Language Center, 1982.

——. "Eyak Texts." *Mimeo.* University of Alaska and Massachusetts Institute of Technology, 1963-1970.

Smelcer, John. *Alaska Native Oral Narrative Literature: A Guidebook and Bibliographic Index.* Anchorage: Ahtna Native Corporation, 1992.

——. *A Cycle of Myths: Native Legends From Southern Alaska.* Anchorage: Salmon Run, 1993.

——. *Eyak and Tsimshian Ethnography: Southeast Alaska Native Oral Narratives in Translation.* Ph.D. Dissertation, 1993.

Haida

Alaska Quarterly Review. Vol. 4, No. 3 & 4. Ed. Tom Sexton, Ron Spatz, and James J. Liszka. Anchorage: University of Alaska Anchorage, 1986.

Barbeau, Marius. *Haida Myths Illustrated in Argillite Carvings.* Ottawa: National Museum of Canada, No. 127, 1953.

Beck, Mary L. *Heroes & Heroines in Tlingit-Haida Legend.* Seattle: Alaska Northwest, 1989.

Bernet, Jack and James Ruppert (eds.) *Our Voices: Stories from Native Alaska and the Yukon.* Lincoln: Nebraska UP, 2001.

Bierhorst, John. *The Mythology of North America.* New York: William Morrow Company, 1985.

Drew, Leslie. *Haida: Their Art and Culture.* Blaire: Hancock House, 1982.

—— and Douglas Wilson. *The Art of the Haida.* Vancouver Hancock House, 1980.

Erdoes, Richard & Alfonso Ortiz (eds). *American Indian Myths and Legends.* New York: Pantheon Book, 1984.

Gridley, Marrion. *The Story of the Haida.* New York: G. P. Putnam's Sons, 1972.

Smelcer, John. *Alaska Native Oral Narrative Literature: A Guidebook and Bibliographic Index.* Anchorage: Ahtna Native Corporation, 1992.

——. *A Cycle of Myths: Native Legends from Southern Alaska.* Anchorage: Salmon Run, 1993.

Swanton, John R. *Contributions to the Ethnology of the Haida.* Washington: American Museum of Natural History, No. 8, 1905.

——. *Haida Texts and Myths.* Washington: Bureau of American Ethnology, Bul. 29, 1905.

—— and Franz Boas. *Haida Songs. Tsimshian Texts.* Washington: American Ethnological Society, Vol. 3, 1912.

Wherry, Joseph H. *Indian Masks and Myths Of The West.* New York: Funk & Wagnell, 1969.

Tlingit

Ackerman, Maria. *Tlingit Stories.* Anchorage: Alaska Pacific University1975.

Alaska Quarterly Review. Vol. 4 No. 3 & 4. Ed. Tom Sexton, Ronald Spatz, James L. Liszka. Anchorage: University of Alaska Anchorage, 1986.

Allen, Henry T. *Report of an Expedition to the Copper, Tanana, and Koyukon Rivers, in the Territory of Alaska, in the Year 1885.* Washington: GPO, 1887.

Beck, Mary L. *Heroes & Heroines in Tlingit-Haida Legend.* Seattle: Alaska Northwest Books, 1989.

———. *Shamans and Kushtakas.* Seattle: Alaska Northwest, 1991.

Bernet, John W., ed. *An Anthology of Aleut, Eskimo, and Indian Literature of Alaska.* Fairbanks: University of Alaska Fairbanks, 1974.

Bernet, Jack and James Ruppert (eds.) *Our Voices: Stories from Native Alaska and the Yukon.* Lincoln: Nebraska UP, 2001.

Carter, M. *Legends, Tales & Totems.* Palmer: Aladdin Press, 1975.

Dauenhauer, Nora and Richard. *Haa Shuka; Our Ancestors.* Juneau: University of Washington Press, 1987.

———. *Haa Tuwunaaqu Yis: For Healing Our Spirit.* Seattle: Washington UP, 1990.

De Laguna, Frederica. *Under Mount Saint Elias: The History and Culture of the Yutat Tlingit.* Washington: Smithsonian, 1972.

Dolch, Edward W. and Marguerite. *Stories From Alaska: Folklore of the World.* Illinois: Garrard Press, 1961.

Dundes, Alan. *Folklore Theses and Dissertations in the United States.* Austin: Texas UP, 1976.

Emmons, George T. *Memoirs of the American Museum of Natural History.* vol. III, 1900-1907.

Erdoes, Richard & Alfonso Ortiz (eds). *American Indian Myths and Legends.* New York: Pantheon Books, 1984.

Fast, Phyllis A. *Naatsilanei and Ko'ehdan: A Semiotic Analysis of Two Alaska Native Myths.* MFA thesis. Anchorage: University of Alaska Anchorage, 1990.

Feldmann, Susan, ed. *The Story-Telling Stone.* New York: Dell, 1965. Reprinted 1991.

Garfield, Viola E. and Linn A. Forest. *The Wolf and the Raven.* Seattle: Washington UP, 1949.

Hallock, Charles. *Our New Alaska.* New York: Forest and Stream Publishing Company, 1886.

Harris, Christie. *Once More Upon A Totem.* New York: Atheneum, 1973.

Harris, Lorie K. *Tlingit Tales.* California: Naturegraph, 1985.

Jonaitis, Aldona. *Art of the Northern Tlingit.* Seattle: Washington UP, 1986.

Jones, Livingston F. *A Study of the Thlingets of Alaska.* New York: Fleming H. Revell, 1914.

Kamenskii, Anatolii. *Tlingit Indians of Alaska.* Trans. Sergei Kan. Fairbanks: University of Alaska Press, 1985.

Kapier, Dan and Nan Kapier. *Tlingit: Their Art, Culture & Legends.* Seattle: Hancock House, 1978.

Keithahn, Edward L. *Monuments in Cedar.* Ketchikan, 1945.

Krause, Aurel. *The Tlingit Indians.* Trans. Erna Gunther. Seattle Washington UP, 1970.

Krenov, Julia. "Legends from Alaska." *Journal de la Societe des Americanistes,* n.s. 40 (1951): 173-95.

Leer, J., ed. *Tongass Texts.* Fairbanks: Alaska Native Language Center, 1978.

Lynch, Kathleen. *Southeastern Stories.* Anchorage: Adult Literacy Laboratory, 1978.

Martin, Fran. *Nine Tales of Raven.* New York: Harper & Row, 1951.

Mayol, Lurline B. *The Talking Totem Pole.* Portland: Binfords & Mort, 1943.

McClellan, Catherine. *The Girl Who Married The Bear: A Masterpiece of Indian Oral Traition.* Ottawa: Canadian National Museum Publication, 1970.

———. "Inland Tlingit." *Subarctic,* vol. 6, 1981.

McCorckle, Ruth. *The Alaska Ten Footed Bear And Other Legends.* Seattle: Robert D. Seal, 1958.

Norman, Howard. *Northern Tales: Traditional Stories of Eskimo and Indian Peoples.* New York: Pantheon. 1990.

Paul, Frances L. *Kahtahah.* Anchorage: Alaska Northwest, 1976.

Peck, Cyrus and Nadja Peck. *The Rocks Of Our Land Speak.* Juneau: Juneau Douglas School District, 1977.

Peck, Cyrus. Sr. *The Tides People.* Juneau: Indian Studies Program. Juneau School District, 1975.

Postell, Alice and A. P. Johnson. *Tlingit Legends.* Sitka: Sheldon Jackson Museum, 1986.

Smelcer, John. *Alaska Native Oral Narrative Literature: A Guidebook and Bibliographic Index*. Anchorage: Ahtna Native Corporation, 1992.

———. *A Cycle of Myths: Native Legends from Southern Alaska*. Anchorage: Salmon Run, 1993.

Swanton, John R. *Tlingit Myths and Texts*. Washington: U. S. Bureau of American Ethology, 1909.

Trask, Willard R. *The Unwritten Song*, vol. II. New York: Macmillan, 1967.

Velten, H. "Three Tlingit Stories." *International Journal of American Linguistics* 10 (1944): 168-180.

Zuboff, Robert. *Kudatan Khaidee (The Salmon Box)*.Trans. Henry Davis. Sitka: Tlingit Readers, Inc., 1973.

———. *Taax'aa (Mosquito)*, ed. and trans Dick Dauenhauer. Fairbanks: A.N.L.C., 1973.

Tsimshian

Angus, Charlotte, et al. *We-Gyet Wanders On: Legends of the Northwest*. Seattle: Hancock House, 1977.

Beynon, William. *Tsimshian Stories*, vols. I-VIII. Metlakatla: Metlakatla Indian Community, 1985.

Bierhorst, John. *The Mythology of North America*. New York: William Morrow Company, 1985.

Boas, Franz. *Tsimshian Texts*. Washington: GPO, Bureau of American Ethnology, Bul. 27, 1902.

———. *Tsimshian Mythology*. Washington: Bureau of American Ethnology, Report 31, 1916.

———. *Tsimshian. Handbook of American Indian Languages*. Bureau of American Ethnology, 1930.

Cove, John. *Shattered Images: Dialogues and Meditations On Tsimshian Narratives*. Ottawa: Carleton UP, 1987.

Garfield, Viola E. and Paul S. Wingert. *The Tsimshian Indians and Their Neighbors of the North Pacific Coast*, eds. Jay Miller and Carol M. Eastman. Seattle: Washington UP, 1950. Reprint, 1966.

McNeary, Stephan A. "Image and Illusion in Tsimshian Mythology." *The Tsimshian and Their Neighbors of the North Pacific Coast*, eds. Jay Miller and Carol M. Eastman. Seattle: Washington UP, 1984.

Niblack, Albert P. *The Coast Indians of Southern Alaska and Northern British Columbia*. Report of the U.S. National Museum, 1890.

Shotridge, L. "A Visit to the Tsimshian Indians." *Museum Journal*, vol. 10. Pennsylvania UP, 1919.

Smelcer, John. *Alaska Native Oral Narrative Literature: A Guidebook and Bibliographic Index.* Anchorage: Ahtna Native Corporation, 1992.

———. *A Cycle of Myths: Native Legends from Southern Alaska.* Anchorage: Salmon Run, 1993.

———. *Eyak and Tsimshian Ethnography: Southeast Alaska Native Oral Narratives in Translation.* Ph.D. Dissertation. 1993.

SOPE: A Tsimshian Story. Anchorage: National Bilingual Materials Development Center, 1978.

Swanton, John R. *Haida Songs. Tsimshian Texts.* Washington: American Ethnological Society, 1912.

Wherry, Joseph H. *Indian Masks and Myths of the West.* New York: Funk & Wagnall, 1969.

About the Authors and Artist

John Smelcer

John Smelcer wearing the bead necklace of the late Ahtna Chief Jim McKinley
and the potlatch vest his grandmother made for him

For more than three years, John Smelcer was the Executive Director of the Ahtna Heritage Foundation, the nonprofit arm of Ahtna Native Corporation tasked with the preservation of Ahtna culture, history,

117

and language. A member of the Ahtna tribe and among the very last speakers of the language, Dr. Smelcer edited, compiled, and published the *Ahtna Noun Dictionary and Pronunciation Guide* (1998, 1999, 2011), which includes forewords by Noam Chomsky and Stephen Pinker. He is also the editor-compiler of the *Alutiiq Noun Dictionary and Pronunciation Guide* (2011), which includes a foreword by the Dalai Lama. John Smelcer is the author numerous novels and of several other collections of Alaska Native myths, including *The Raven and the Totem* and *A Cycle of Myths*. With Joseph Bruchac, Dr. Smelcer co-edited *Native American Classics* (2013), a graphic anthology of 19th and early 20th century Native American literature. His popular Alaska-themed novels include *The Trap, The Great Death, Lone Wolves, Edge of Nowhere* and *Savage Mountain*. Dr. Smelcer's education includes postdoctoral studies at Cambridge, Oxford, and Harvard.

Gary Snyder

Gary Snyder won the Pulitzer Prize in 1975 for his book *Turtle Island*. The author of dozens of books of poetry and prose, including books on Native American mythology, he has been a Guggenheim Fellow and a member of the American Academy of Arts and Letters. He received the Ruth Lilly Poetry Prize from the Poetry Foundation in 2008. He is a professor of English at the University of California at Davis.

Larry Vienneau

Larry Vienneau had three pieces selected as Finalists and one was a winner in *The Artist's Magazine*'s 2011 28th Annual International Art Competition. He lives in Florida and is a Professor of Art at Seminole State College. For many years, he was a professor of art at the University of Alaska-Fairbanks, where he met John Smelcer. Larry has exhibited in the North America, South America, Europe, and Asia and has won awards in national and international competitions. His prints are intaglio etching on paper. The "Raven Series" began in 1992 as illustrations for this book, but he has since continued to explore the images associated with this incredible bird.

CPSIA information can be obtained
at www.ICGtesting.com
Printed in the USA
FFOW02n1947140216
21483FF